HIDDEN IN TIME

An Elven Heritage Novel

CHRISSY WISSLER

Blue Cedar Publishing

ALSO BY CHRISSY WISSLER

Elven Heritage Series

Hidden in Mist

Hidden in Truth

Hidden in Shadow

Hidden in Fire

Hidden in Flight

Hidden in Spirit

Hidden in Desire

Hidden in Memory

Hidden in Time Novel

Hidden in Lore: Collection #1

Hidden in Myth: Collection #2

Hidden in Legend: Collection #3

Hidden in Darkness: Free Story

Little League Series

Swing Away: A Little League Novel

Prom Dates & Softball Bats

Throw Like a Girl, Catch a Date

Fly Away

No Crying in Softball

More to Life than Softball

A Pitcher's Unexpected Date

A Catcher's Christmas Wish

Stolen Bases, Stolen Kisses

ACKNOWLEDGMENTS

This story couldn't have been written without the willing (and sometimes not so willing) cooperation of my family. For Sean, who watched the kids while I carved out this time for myself. For Kate and Eric who gave me the quiet and space to actually dive down into the characters and tell this story. And, well, for myself for doing what was needed to get to the writing each day, several times a day, with all the demands of parenthood and the unique gifts and path of our family. The push to actually write this story, to tell the next bit of Kate Silver's story, definitely goes to Dean Wesley Smith who offered up a novel writing challenge—and I accepted. This challenge gave me the grit I needed to get back into writing novels despite this season my life is in (re: young kids and very little sleep).

To Kate and Eric—
For teaching me what true strength looks like.

Kate took another slow step, her hiking boots pressing into the soft, spongy grass. She shivered as a cooling breeze drifted up and around the tall trunks of pine trees and larches and a whole bunch of others whose names she didn't know (and frankly, didn't care a whole lot about either).

She wanted to stay.

To sit on that boulder right there, overlooking that slow-moving creek, with water that had a hint of aqua to it. Fresh and cold from all the glaciers melting way off and up there in the distance, nestled up in those dark mountain peaks. She'd sprawl, arms and legs stretched out on that rock, with its mix of pink and black and ruddy-brown specks. Close her eyes. Feel the last bit of warmth from both the rock and the sun until, finally, she fell into a comfortable, peaceful rest.

After all, it *had* been a long, long three days of hiking. Camping. Trudging up some mountain in the middle of nowhere Montana, in the middle of July, sweat pouring out of just about every pore, all to help her understand her heritage.

Oh, and totally skipping on the showering bit. Or the simple washing of her hair.

Ugh.

Her hair *used* to be this darker blond color, nice sunlight gold streaks, about the only attractive feature. Now though... well, her hair looked more like the forest floor, what with all the twigs and leaves and tangles she'd acquired since she'd started this oh-so-lovely camping expedition into the wilderness of Alfeim.

And yet, even with her missing all those oh, so important amenities, she wanted to stay.

Stay right here, in this small glade with its trickling creek and canopy of pine needles, the way the trees and their branches bowed to her, their bark and joints creaking as if they'd been asleep for an age, but finally, because of her, were waking up.

The glade didn't want her to go either.

She felt it.

Felt the trees, who were sad to see her leave. Even the grass, somehow still holding onto moisture from the morning dew all those hours ago, and how the heck there was any moisture at all was certainly some kind of magic (she had the sweat-soaked T-shirt to prove just how damn hot and dry it got during the day). That grass though, magic or not, with all its small individual blades, gave her a final, wet tickling along her ankles, right where her wool socks couldn't quite reach.

The last of the setting sun cast a dusting of gold specks in the air as if it, too, were waving goodbye.

Above her, circling high up overhead in the hot thermals and wind currents, was Eagle. His great brown wings stretched out as he rode the hot thermals and wind currents of that endless sky, with all those purples and pinks blending until finally fading into darkness.

Simply beautiful. All of it.

Kate breathed in, feeling the peace of this place, the peace she was finally feeling within herself. About her unique heritage. About the warm, new candlelight glowing within her.

And there, right in the middle of that endless sky, stretching out across the whole it seemed, was Eagle. His brilliant white head a beacon, ready to lead her home.

Eagle gave a sad, shrill cry.

He knew her well, her spirit guide. Always there for her, always watching out for her. And now, telling her it was time to leave.

Kate's stomach twisted.

Just a little, but enough. Enough to know that, by taking this one last step, she'd be leaving a part of herself behind.

Which, in a way, she was.

This wasn't her glade, exactly. It was Kátheryn's.

Kátheryn Silverstar, the warm candlelight within her.

The soft pink and gold flame. Still small, just like an actual candle flame, but growing stronger. And Kate had a feeling that the real Kátheryn probably felt more like a high school bonfire.

But now, more than ever, Kate understood why she'd always felt so different. So weird and strange.

She *was* different. Yes, she was an elf-descendant, just like her mom, just like her grandma, and also, a bit more. Like, an actual elven soul living right beside hers.

That's right. Not just one, but two souls.

Cause her life couldn't get anymore complicated with it just being *her* in there.

Her, the recently-turned seventeen-year-old who'd been seen as odd and weird everywhere she went, every house she'd lived in, every school she'd been forced into. The reaction, the treatment, by her classmates, teachers too, always the same. Her slightly pointed ears and crazy-good hearing really didn't help. Then there was her mom, Queen of Denial and Running, who'd pretty much dumped her out in the wilds of Montana with a crazy Grandma who, while she was crazy, had a certain fondness for shotguns and a history that you'd never, ever find in history books.

Like tales straight out of myths. Probably legends, if you believed in that sort of thing.

Like... well, like Kátheryn.

Kátheryn Silverstar who was the other part of Kate, the part that had *really* made her seem 'other' to just about every person she met. Except for Grandma. And James.

Kátheryn, the long-dead elf soul whose glade Kate now stood in.

This place had once been her home... a really, really long time ago, but it was pretty apparent that the glade, and the trees, probably even the ants crawling up that branch not two inches from her head, remembered her.

Kátheryn, that was.

Not Kate.

And she had to leave. Had to leave this beautiful, peaceful place. A place where she could well and truly hide, where all the bad things out there couldn't get her, from her evil-ass dad to the sore heart she just knew she'd feel the second she caught a glimpse of James again.

Because... she had to get back to camp. To warn Grandma about James's bitch of a mom and the war she wanted to start between the magi and the elf-descendants. A warning Kate had gotten because of Kátheryn and her magic, and the memory from Alfeim Forest itself.

There was still so much Kate didn't know about her heritage, about who she was, or heck, even what she could do. And Kátheryn, she'd shown Kate just a little bit more. How to connect with Alfeim Forest, its consciousness, to feel the actual shifting of the earth as it breathed, the small worms and bugs digging down there amidst the roots. And by doing so, she'd been able to see the forest Memory. A memory as if she'd been standing right there, watching the whole thing unfold.

A memory and a warning, one that she needed to share. She had to tell James, even if he'd end up hating her for it.

Eagle called to her again. Urging her and a little... uneasy it felt like. Like he needed her to move. To hurry.

Yes, it was time to go.

"I'm sorry," Kate whispered.

Though, she didn't know if she spoke to the glade or that slight tightening in her chest. An ache that she felt like it was splitting her in two.

Not that she could blame Kátheryn. After all, just waking up from a really long sleep and learning the person whose eyes you stared out was actually a pretty pathetic version of an elf-descendant, who was bad at just about *everything* elvish.

Like magic.

Especially magic.

Which was just another truth she couldn't run from. Not any

longer. Couldn't be her mom, who just kept running and driving and hiding. Oh, and lots of denying.

Not Kate. Never, Kate.

At least, not anymore.

Eagle flew on ahead, straight into that sunset. Kate followed him, followed the golden strand that always connected them. She took one last look at the glade, this place that felt like home and called to just about every inch of her being. The sun finished its descent, giving her one last, golden wink.

She took that final step—

Her boots sank straight down into a giant mound of freezing, brilliant white snow. And her connection to Eagle, her beautiful spirit guide, with his constant warmth and love, who believed in her when no one would, snapped.

CHAPTER TWO

Eagle was gone.

The hot summer of July where she'd sweated out about every ounce of water she'd drunk, gone.

The snow immediately swallowed her boots whole, falling down her socks, past her laces. That numbing tingling feeling, it hit her so hard and fast. The power it had—snow, the cold, all of it—set her teeth chattering in a whole 1.5 seconds.

Lips ready to turn blue.

And the rest of the snow mound, well, it decided to tag along for the ride since she was apparently standing in a snow pile that went up to her knees. Her *bare* knees because she was wearing ripped-up jeans. Her *bare* arms because she was swearing a thin, sweat-soaked T-shirt. Modest enough, too. Within the appropriate range, anyway. Her grandma, after all, was nearby. With her shotgun, mind you. At least, she had been.

Four months ago.

Shit.

Kate slapped her hands around her arms, and bounced up and down right where she stood. Snow falling into more little nooks and crannies of her boots, her jeans, places she had no idea snow could get to.

Freezing didn't begin to cover what she was feeling.

Or the fear.

Because one step ago, it *had* been July and this here, this snow that she was standing in, and the wind which took clumps of it and threw it right in her face, was most clearly, most definitely, no not July.

And Eagle—she couldn't feel him. Couldn't sense him. She'd... never been apart from him, not since she first learned who she was, what she was.

Panic started to take hold. She spun in a circle, searching the gray sky, but saw nothing but falling white.

"Eagle—"

The wind swallowed her voice.

Ate it, more like.

And Kátheryn? She could barely sense Kátheryn's flame, suddenly so dim and dull, almost like she wasn't there at all.

All around her, the same trees that had just been bowing their branches towards her, bending and creaking like they'd been stretching out their long limbs from a super-deep slumber, were completely silent. And completely covered in heavy piles of that same brilliant-white snow. It looked like Elsa herself had come on out here and just went all frozen on everything. Like she'd iced over the whole world and all that remained were the sculptures of trees trying to escape. Trying to get help.

Trying... to get Kate?

She shivered so hard her teeth chattered. The wind tugged at her hair, the ponytail and all the bits of branches and leaves she'd collected since Grandma had made her come on this stupid hike, but that now made her heart ache because Grandma wasn't here.

The ends of her hair had already started to ice over, like Elsa really was standing right next to her.

Not to mention the zero feeling she had in her hands.

She was certainly *not* in Kansas anymore. But snow?

Snow?

What the hell was going on? And more importantly, how was she going to survive another five minutes?

Kate felt it then, a slight tingling along her senses. So dull, though, she'd almost missed it with the high-clattering going on of her teeth.

There was something wrong.

Yes, well, clearly.

Kate gripped her arms even tighter and took another stumbling, sinking step forward and got a mouthful of snow and ice for the effort.

But the awareness of the other part of her, of her elven heritage and Kátheryn herself, it stayed. Dull, yes, but there. And as much as she could, especially as the cold stole energy and warmth and life right out of her body... she tried to focus.

Focused outwards. Focused beyond that freezing cold, to see with more than just her eyes, to feel more than just her skin...

She couldn't do it. Couldn't.

She was freezing. Too much. Too cold.

The candlelight within her glowed, a warm pink and gold, then suddenly dulled. Kate almost felt Kátheryn's solemn nod urging her to move. Quickly. To save herself.

"No... shit..." Kate chattered.

Not that she could move very far, or very well. She stumbled up and out of that snow mound, only to face another, this one reaching her hips. Soft-packed snow, fucking freezing snow, but still really, really hard to push through, like she was shoving her way through quicksand.

Her thoughts, already, were tumbling out of control. Giving way to the cold. To the numbness.

Kátheryn and her candlelight stayed with her, though so very weak. Nothing at all like she'd been in her glade, the strength Kate had felt for her, the trust she'd put into the elven soul. Something had happened. Something bad.

Didn't matter. Not now.

Just kept focusing... one foot... in front of the other. Moving forward. Past the frozen larches with their leaves, their *golden* leaves, frozen straight up in and encased in a whole lot of ice.

Again came that tingling of awareness.

And if Kate were in her right mind, you know, not freezing to death, she'd have stopped and pondered this strangeness. The kind of strangeness that only occurred when magic stepped into play, but since she was trying to simply stay alive, she filed the thought away to ponder at a later date.

For now, one step. Then another.

Fire? Could she make it?

Nope, not a chance in hell.

Shelter first, right?

Her idea of shelter was a fluffy warm blanket and an electric heater. Both, nowhere in sight.

Dear god, she didn't know the first thing about survival. Or camping. Or anything to do with nature. Again, her mom's fault. But what had Grandma been thinking, bringing her out here in the middle of nowhere? As if *that* would simply turn on the light bulb in her and she'd be more elf-descendant worthy and all that crap, instead of who she actually was.

The girl who'd made mistake after mistake. Like how she'd gone walking off on her own, leaving camp and the safety of Grandma (and her shotgun) behind. To be fair, they'd *told* her to leave and get firewood and all that (only the dead kind; Kate had very specific instructions about *not* pissing off the temperamental, magical forest). Which was when she'd gotten snatched up by Eolis

Her mind thought about the name for a moment.

Eolis.

A memory triggered. The former human, turned elf, with his threadbare clothes and piercing gray eyes—

Wait. Eolis.

He'd been there. In the glade. He'd witnessed Kate and Kátheryn working together to view the forest's Memory. And then he'd left only moments before she and Eagle had.

Hope burned, hot and powerful.

Maybe... maybe he was here too?

Kate shoved past the snow, turning back in the direction of the glade, only a few steps away where she'd be safe again, maybe even back by that sun-warmed boulder—

Except, no Eolis in sight.

No glade, either.

Like they'd both simply disappeared.

The creek? The boulder with the black and pink specks she'd fantasized falling asleep on? All gone.

Disappeared, like magic.

Now there was only this open field of snow. Lots and lots of snow. A snow so deep in parts she could only see the end tips of trees, like whitecake toppers. Then there was the wind throwing bits of it this way and that, causing the small snowflakes and ice crystals to sting her eyes, which, come to think of it, was good. She still had feeling there as well.

She was alone. Totally and completely alone.

Except for Kátheryn, who Kate could barely feel.

Again came that tugging. The awareness, just there, right beyond her thoughts.

Kátheryn's warm light glowing, just a bit brighter.

All Kate had to do was let go and *trust*…

Except… wasn't that what she'd just done?

She'd trusted Kátheryn when they'd used her magic together to see that Memory, and now she was in three feet of snow, in the middle of Elsa's ice kingdom.

Trust was really, really hard to do when she'd lost feeling of her toes.

Kate's teeth clanked. The shivers now were so hard, so uncontrollable, it felt like she was going to break into a thousand tiny bits and shards. Fingers, nose, toes: all numb.

And then, just nothing. Nothing at all. No pain, just numbness.

She found herself on her knees, snow all around her, and wondered, with slowing, dull thoughts, how she'd gotten there.

Snow that suddenly seemed to fall faster and faster from the gray, cloud-filled sky. The snow, the ice, it kept on swirling, kept stinging like the sharpest needles imaginable until she couldn't even feel that.

Had to keep thinking… had to focus… had to…

Couldn't.

Not when there were bits of blue lightning sparking around. Almost, singing in the air. Snap and zap. Closer and closer.

Maybe it was her eyes playing tricks on her.

Probably.

Or maybe it was a sign that she was totally screwed.

Most likely.

And somehow, even through all numbness, when she could barely breathe because her lungs, her whole body was suddenly so numb, the act of simply taking in air felt like too much effort, too much weight to lift up, and then down again with an exhale.

Through all that, her mind found clarity. Or a little bit, anyway.

Kate had stepped into Kátheryn's glade, a place that had been warm with sunset and light of July, had accepted the part of herself that was Kátheryn and in doing so, they'd been able to see a Memory of Alfeim Forest. A Memory that had warned her about James and his mom, Aila, and her really, really not nice plans for Kate.

A Memory Kate was able to see because of magic...

Magic.

Elven magic.

A kind she barely understood and had even less control over. And the moment she'd walked out of the glade, she'd found herself in the middle of winter.

As if she'd lost a few months.

Of time.

Kate had used the magic that allowed her to see a moment in time. A time that had passed, yes, except... it had been so real. She'd been able to *taste* that sharp bite of snow on her skin, the cold that was so piercing it felt like every sense combined into one until it was all that existed. All that she felt.

Sorta like now.

But... the Memory, standing there, witnessing it unfold... it had been real. Like she'd been right beside Aila and her evil dad as they discussed the nasty plans they had for her. For this world. For the vanished elves.

Except... she'd done this. She'd caused this. Not her dad. Not Aila.

Her.

The cold seeped deeper into her until it was all that remained. Her thoughts broke away, one by one. The clarity she felt vanished into the wind like all those thousands of swirling snowflakes and bits of blue lightning.

But not completely.

"Oh, no." Her mouth barely moving, voice barely more than a whispered grunt. "What the hell did I do this time?"

"A damn, damn fine question," said gruff voice behind her. "One I think can wait a spell, don't ya think?"

CHAPTER THREE

Kate tried for a scream. A movement to defend herself, like flailing hands or throwing her shoe, anything, to keep some guy she hadn't seen, hadn't heard, away from her. (Some freakin' amazing elf-descendant she was. It was a *good* thing Grandma was nowhere near; she'd rip Kate a new one at being so damn careless. Again.)

Of course, Kate couldn't defend herself. Or move, actually. Or think, for that matter.

But she really did give it her best effort.

She pushed off her knees and fell completely into the snow. Clouds of it sprang up into the air, swirled and danced around her. She shoved as best she could with feet and toes she couldn't feel, scrambling backwards, anything to get away from him...

And moved a whole two inches.

She could almost hear him laughing at her, the deep barrel sound of his chest, echoing round and round in that swirling snow and lightning. Or maybe it wasn't him laughing. Maybe it was the forest and all that wind and snow. She also couldn't quite see because of that storm, just a giant, dark form that towered over her.

Towered. Like, bigger than those trees half-buried in the snow and ice field. Big hands on his hips, and him shaking his head like he was just as disappointed as Grandma always with her every time Kate opened her mouth or made a mistake (which felt like always).

Kate had learned enough out here, as she set out on this ridiculous (it seemed) path to understand herself, her heritage—to not trust anyone. And to believe that, pretty much, everything and everyone was out to get her.

Including a giant-sized man who finally stopped shaking his head and walked through that snowstorm like he was parting the Red Sea or something. And the entire storm, lightning included, suddenly stopped. That's right. Stopped right there, mid-flash, snow hanging there as if frozen in time.

Oh, dear lord.

He was also as big as she'd first thought. He had at least a good two feet on her, and it wasn't like she was short to begin with. His beard was covered with so much snow she hadn't a clue what color it was. But that's not what held her attention.

It was the eye-patch, looking just like you'd expect from some pirate king sailing the high seas. And you didn't exactly see eye-patches or pirates, even out here in Montana (shotgun totting grannies—yes, but no pirates). But it was the scar, the one that she could tell cut right down through where his eye would have been—that's what held her attention.

And the other eye, the one that seemed to swirl with just about every color imaginable, as he glared at her. Annoyed, for sure.

"Who... who, what?"

It was all her frozen lips and lungs could manage.

"You done?" he asked.

He didn't wait for an answer. Just took two steps with his giant-ass legs and hauled her up. Yep. Hauled her up by the back of her neck like she was some kitten in serious trouble by mom.

"Cause right now, we don't got time for your nagging questions and what not. Unless you'd like to just lay back down right where I found you?"

She managed to shake her head.

At least, she thought she did.

He huffed. "Makin' me wait out here. It's cold, you know. Hell, not even knowin' when you'd hop out of that bubble there. Shit. About ready to give up myself."

The more he talked, the more the feeling from earlier came back. Not the feeling in her toes, but that sense of something off, of... *other*...

Kátheryn, though, her and her candlelight flame, were still too dim, too dull to help Kate see, to help her understand.

Something more...

The man's eye continued to swirl and spark with colors (he did seem pretty mad at her), and she had the strangest feeling that she knew him. Or that she'd seen him before. Or maybe it was her well and truly losing all feeling in her body. That was entirely possible.

The man shoved aside a bunch of snow that had somehow fallen on top of her and swore.

He did that a lot. Reminded her, very clearly, of Grandma.

"Shit," he said. "What the hell you wearin'? I told Emmaline to get you proper and ready."

Kate tried to talk, tried to whisper the one word she so desperately wanted to: Grandma?

Grandma knew him? Grandma had sent him? Was Grandma... was she here?

Course, all that actually happened was her passing out.

FEELING CAME BACK TO KATE, all of her, in a single, painful moment. It was like one moment, nothing but darkness, a relief really after what she'd just been through, walking out a nice glade in the middle of July to a snowstorm swirling with snow and ice and blue lightning.

Clearly, magic was involved, and clearly, at least some of it was her fault.

Again.

But there she went from one moment of resting in this blissful blackness to a burn that shot through her so hard, so fast, and so incredibly painful it felt like it was eating her alive. Searing right through her. Chest, nose, arms and legs—nothing was spared. Not even fingers and toes. It was like all her nerves decided in one moment —together—they needed to come back alive... and tell her just how damn close she'd been to dying.

Apparently, quite close.

Kate woke up from that darkness. She flung out her arms, the ones that hurt, the fingers that felt like they were alive with zapping electricity. She pushed away the heavy, wonderfully warm blankets and furs.

Oh, dear god, did she hurt.

And oh, wow, did it feel glorious.

Except for realizing she was totally and completely naked.

She grabbed those furs and shoved herself—and her toes—back under them. Which she'd have done anyway because it was really, really warm.

Kate closed her eyes for a moment.

Needed to simply breathe. She was alive. Alive.

And with that realization, her mind, the rational, thinking part of her, started coming back online. Pushed through the pain as her body woke up from its near-frozen sleep enough to start giving her advice and putting the clues together.

Wet clothes. Hypothermia.

Yes, she knew enough that they had to go. That's why she was naked; no other reason.

And she was clearly taken care of. Brought to this warm place and these warm blankets, rather quickly since she was, after all, still alive.

She opened her eyes and saw that, yes, while it felt like her body was on fire, there was an actual, wonderfully really (and hot) fire just a few feet from her. A fire sitting in an actual fireplace with misshapen black rocks holding the whole thing up, nothing fancy like you'd see in some ski resort, but dear lord, did it do the trick.

There was also a heavy black pot above it. Tea kettle, too. She hoped their presence meant food. Certainly smelled like food, and really, really yummy, too. The steam coming out the top carried the scent of beef and garlic, and her mouth immediately watered.

Her stomach followed suit with a very loud, very distinct rumble.

If her host hadn't heard her flailing around upon waking, he certainly would be aware now.

And... she wasn't afraid at the thought. Sometime between meeting him in that snow and blue lightning storm, passing out, and now, her subconscious had reached a decision about him. Sure, she was alive, but then a person like her dad or even Aila wouldn't mind keeping her alive either, so long as it meant they'd get what they wanted.

But the gruff mountain man knew Grandma. Hell, he even *sounded* like Grandma.

The cabin—at least it appeared to be a cabin—was wall-to-ceiling sandy-brown wood, and it was plastered with so many different kinds of furs it'd probably have made her mother faint (and make her grandmother proud). Right now, Kate was just super grateful for their presence, so heavy and warm and wrapped around her just so. Even better, when she tried, her toes actually wiggled on command. All ten of them.

Fingers, too.

Thank god, indeed.

"Huh. Imagine that," the gruff voice said. "Didn't expect you to come about so quickly. Maybe you're not a total loss."

Kate pushed up to her elbows, careful cause it really still did hurt, and turned to look at him.

The man was as tall as she'd first guessed. Either that, or it was a really, really tiny cabin. Even sitting down in that rickety rocking chair, smoking a pipe about as long as her arm, his head practically brushed the ceiling. A gray head and a grey beard, and more scars than she'd ever seen on a person. It looked more like a roadmap than an actual face. Furs wrapped about him, no fancy, synthetic jacket from the North Face or some other high-tech brand. Just furs and leather. Not to mention the leather boots and the brilliant white fur lining round the cuff.

He looked like he'd stepped out of some long-gone century. One of those mountain men who spent their winters where not even hell dared go, trapping animals and what not, and selling it to the people cozied up in their cities much, much further down south.

And unlike earlier, when she was passing out due to freezing to death, his single eye was not a swirl of changing colors. Instead his eye was a hazel-like green that stared down at her so intense she well and truly did feel naked. Not because she actually was naked (minus the fur blankets), but that he saw straight through to her soul.

Both of them.

And he was pretty darn unhappy with both of them.

It was hard to not fidget. Shit, did he make her feel like Grandma.

Kate cleared her throat. "I umm... thank you. I wanted to thank you."

He said nothing. Just continued to stare at her.

"You know, for saving my life. Out there. In the snow."

"Is that what I did, Kátheryn Silverstar?"

Kate flushed. "I don't know. I mean, I don't know if *she* knows, because, well... it's not like she's talking to me or anything."

"No. No, course not. Cause being upfront and honest like that don't bode well for your kind, do it Kátheryn?"

"Look. She's not here. I mean, she's not the one sitting here, talking to you. I don't even know if she's awake—"

"She is."

"Well, fine. Then I'll take a moment later to deal with *her*, and on my own terms, thanks very much. But right now, I have no idea what you're talking about or who you are or how you know my grandmother."

He pulled the pipe out of his mouth. A puff of smoke blew out his nose. For a second, he almost looked like a dragon, a rumbling one that wasn't sure if he wanted to lose his temper, eat her, or laugh good, loud, and hard.

Either way, it was pissing her off.

"Emmaline," he said finally, "was right 'bout one thing. You got spark. Spark's good. Probably the only reason you've survived so long."

He shook his head. Long gray hair hung over his ears, so she couldn't tell if they had the slight point like her and all the other elf-descendants. But pointy ears or not... he was someone who wouldn't harm her.

Someone, someone she could trust.

"Your ma did you no favors," he said, "keepin' the truth from you, and Emmaline, shit, she didn't do much better. Takin' you and throwin' you by your ankles into the deep end. It's a wonder you didn't drown. A marvel, actually."

She took it back about trusting him.

Instead, she wanted to throttle him.

Kate tugged the blankets tighter around her chest. Actually, she wanted to thrust her finger and jab it right into his chest. Thirty seconds with the guy and she was ready to give *him* a talking to. It wasn't like she'd survived this long by accident. She'd stood up to her evil dad when he'd attempted to kidnap her. She'd managed to talk Alfeim Forest down when it was really pissed off at her and thought she'd make a nice tasty snack.

She'd done all that, all of it, on her own. No elf soul to guide her or boost her up with some kind of magic. No help or guidance from anyone, not even Grandma. Okay, so she did have Eagle there—*had*—Eagle. The thought ripped right through. She nearly sank right back down into the bed with how hard and fast her heart was suddenly pounding.

Eagle.

She took a deep, steadying breath. One problem at a time.

First, she was alive and with all appendages in working order. And she'd survived that snowy field. Once again, survived. Just as she'd done when she'd crossed the freakin' veil. She'd done what no other elf-descendant could, or dared, and walked right into that misty, between place. The place that separated her world from all the others.

She'd done that. Kate Silver.

And she'd survived. So like hell was she going to let some dude she didn't know, even as big as he was, tell her what she could and could not do.

"You know what?" Kate said. "Grandma may have thrown me in, deep end or not, but I swam."

Not well, but she'd done it.

"I did not drown."

He huffed. "Didn't you?"

"No."

Except... it was his huff that got to her.

That, and the sense from before, back in the snowy field among the

Elsa-like frozen trees, and all those the trapped golden leaves... leaves that would have been that color in *fall* and not the middle of winter.

Kate swallowed.

She'd done something, changed something when she'd used Kátheryn's magic to see a Memory. She'd gone back in time, even if only to see what Alfeim Forest had seen, had witnessed, and had *wanted* Kate to see as well...

Again... that tingling just beyond reach...

But Kátheryn remained a barely burning flame. The warning wasn't coming from her.

But something was seriously not right. And it wasn't just stepping out of a warm glade with the echoes of the creek all around her and walking straight into winter.

No... something... something else.

She remembered her thought from earlier, her thought about time itself...

Kate pushed herself up on the bed until she was sitting cross-legged, pulling the blankets even closer. The coarse, black fur tickled her chin. Behind her, the warm fire comforted her, but not nearly enough because right now, it felt like her insides had suddenly frozen over.

Kate looked right at the mountain man with his furs and gray beard, his eye-patch, and the scars lining every inch of his face. He was testing her, all right, seeing if she would run. If she was afraid.

Well, she was. Didn't mean she couldn't do anything about it.

"What aren't you telling me?"

He took another long puff on his pipe. Said nothing.

Kate wanted to throw that fur blanket at him. Didn't, if only for modesty's sake.

"What?" she demanded.

"Magic. What else."

Oh man, was she seconds from chucking the whole bed at him, her being naked or not.

"You are about as cryptic as Grandma ever was," Kate said, "and that's seriously not helping."

He laid his pipe down across his knees. The smoke from both the pipe and the cooking pot seemed to blend above him, come together, and for a brief moment, she thought she saw the sparks. The faintest traces of blue lightning... and the unmistakable shift as his eye went from dull green to brilliant purple.

"Magic," his voice rumbled. Rumbled so deep, in fact, the whole cabin seemed to shake.

She just kept staring, right back at him. Refused to look away.

Finally, he nodded.

"Magic," he said again, "that you used, that you had no business usin' or touching or anything of the like. And that elf in you, Kátheryn Silverstar, knew better."

Kátheryn, as if straight-up reacting to this man and his presence, dimmed even further. As if... she were afraid of him. Or, had a really, really healthy dose of wariness.

And that made Kate wary.

A little, anyway.

But not enough to back down and hide. To run. She was *not* her mother.

"What did I do?"

He stared at her for another moment, that eye of his shifting from purple to blue to green. And she sat there and took it, every inch of that gaze as it raked right through her, seeing more than she knew possible. All the ugly parts of her. Her fears, her stubbornness, and the real reason she made so many mistakes, was so *bad* at anything resembling a great elf-descendant of old, was because of her own refusal, her own stubbornness. Because even now, part of her didn't fully believe.

In what she was, or in what she did.

"I won't run," Kate whispered. "I know it had to do with time, I'm not stupid. Tell me. Please."

She didn't look away when she said 'please,' either.

He simply nodded. "Yes. You used a forbidden magic. Time magic. You used time to look backwards, and in return, it cost a year of your life. It cost all of us a year."

CHAPTER FOUR

Kate had been expecting something along the lines of, 'Well, it's a real shame what you did there, because you know, the past is in the past and that's exactly where it should stay. And cause you went and screwed up (again) you fast-forwarded time by a month. Oops. Don't do it again.'

And, of course, a really big emphasis on the 'again.'

But a year?

A *year*?

The heat of the fire, the comforting warmth of the blankets, this closed-in little cabin, all of it, suddenly felt like too much. Felt like she was trapped and couldn't... couldn't quite breathe.

Or maybe it was the way her head was suddenly spinning and the room was starting to tilt a bit too much to the left.

"Lay down," the gruff, mountain man snapped at her. "I ain't pickin' your naked ass off the floor if you faint."

But regardless of what he said, he did reach for her, almost as if he cared... or maybe he didn't want his obviously nice furs all over the dust-covered floor. Funny how she hadn't noticed that little detail beforehand, like this cabin hadn't been used for a long, long time.

Weird how the mind picks up little details like that.

"Lay down, Kate."

She felt his hand—rough yes, but surprisingly gentle—lead her back to the bed. Gentle, until she resisted.

"No, no. I'm not just going to lay back down and sleep after you just laid *that* on me."

She gripped his arm in return, her fingers still painful, the nerves there still frying up, still coming back to life after her near-miss of losing the whole lot.

Best not to think about that. Couldn't control the past or what she'd done. What she *could* do was understand... and figure out how not do that in the future, along with *why* Kátheryn thought the risk so important just to show Kate just that memory. And why *that* memory? Why not something more important like, what the hell had happened to her, to all the elves in the first place?

Chances were it'd cost Kate her entire life to know the answer to that one. Still, she tucked the thought away for another time.

First things first. Starting with what she could handle.

"Who are you?" Kate asked again. "No dodging. Don't think I didn't notice you haven't told me yet."

He pulled back, his one eye settling back to that dull green color, but believe her, there was nothing dull about this man, much as he tried to hide it. Or mask it.

Jesus, it was like he was a living body of magic. She glanced again at his ears, but no, the long gray hair was seriously, perfectly arranged just so she couldn't see their shape.

He grinned at her, as if he knew exactly what she was trying to determine. It was like he could almost read her mind. No kidding, his grin widened just at that moment, showing her fairly straight, somewhat white, but certainly menacing teeth. Like there really were two sides to this man, the grinning side, and the side that, like Alfeim Forest, had no issue eating you if you got in his way.

A seriously disturbing thought.

"Who *are* you?" she asked.

"I go by a couple names out here. One-Eye. Hawk-Eye. All-Seeing-Eye. Eagle-Eye."

"I meant an actual name. Not a code name."

Or a superhero from the Marvel comics.

Again, the grin.

And, no answer.

Kate crossed her arms. "What did *Grandma* call you?"

"Well... she had a few names for me as well, the old bat, most of which ain't appropriate for a young lady such as yourself. Or come to think of it, weren't much appropriate for her neither, but then your grandmother never cared much for those social niceties and all."

This time, it was Kate's turn give *him* the stink-eye.

He laughed. It filled the whole room, joyous and so full she could almost picture him sitting around a great table with great men, raising their goblets and gauntleted hands in glorious toasts while spinning tales and adventures of old.

She shook her head. Where had *that* thought come from?

"You are indeed Emmaline's mirror." He quieted, though the mirth did not leave his eyes.

Err... eye.

"I will give you my name, at least the one she called me by, when not swearing at me, which was often. I am Durlan Greybeard, and I am the one who your grandmother asked for help when she realized what you'd done, though she was not the one to reach me first."

Uh... okay.

She might finally have a name, but Kate couldn't shake the feeling that there was way more that he wasn't telling her. As if she hadn't noticed how his country-bumpkin speech suddenly changed... and once again, the image popped into her head of a glorious table, a great feast set forth for those who were righteous and worthy.

Ugh. She really, really should have asked more questions from Grandma about the elves, and especially the place they originally came from. Cause this guy here, he was way, way more than he seemed.

Kátheryn was certainly keeping her mouth shut. Though it probably had a lot to do with Durlan Graybeard and that crazy magic that seemed to spark off him, and the look he was giving her.

Or, Kátheryn.

But honestly, Kate really, really wanted to have this conversation.

She wanted to hear exactly what happened, both what she did and what happened during the whole year... *year?*

Kate swallowed the really hard, really big lump in her throat.

At which point her stomach growled, reminding her there were other things she needed. Like food. Not to mention dry (and warm) clothes back on. Oh, and please, please wash her face. Maybe even brush her teeth—

Durlan stood, the rocker scraping along the hard, dusty floor. "I will be outside."

"Huh?"

"You are hungry. You wish to dress and wash."

"I don't have any clothes." Except her jeans and T-shirt. "Suitable clothes."

He nodded at a wooden chest, which was practically hidden in the room because it was the same color as the wood floor and walls.

"Clothes. As I said, I was expecting you."

As much as she wanted food, she couldn't help it. She needed to know the answer to just one more question.

"You said someone else had found you, before Grandma did."

Durlan nodded.

"Well, aren't you going to tell me?"

His grin, his mirth, all of it, disappeared. Grim resolution gazed at her, and his single eye switched to purple again, so purple it was nearly black.

"You know him well. Both you and Kátheryn."

Kate's breath trapped in her throat. She didn't know if it was her reaction, or Kátheryn's.

"James," she whispered.

"James. He found me. Sent me to find the right time, right place. Bring you back, if I could."

His gaze, all one-eye of it, never left her.

"I couldn't." His ruffled gray hair brushed the cabin's ceiling as he moved. "I will wait outside. Dress. Clean. Eat."

Durlan grabbed some heavier, thicker, bulkier jacket from along the wall where he'd hung it. Then, with a mighty heave the door opened—

shooting a blast and flurry of snow and ice—and then banged shut behind him.

If anyone had abrupt exits, it was her, but in this case she really, really didn't mind.

Because all of a sudden she couldn't think again or move. The one word echoing in her mind, again and again.

James.

CHAPTER FIVE

Kate was sitting on the bed again, fur blankets tucked about her as she sat cross-legged. The warm pants she now wore, synthetic and stretchy, were a perfect fit. In fact, so were the clean underwear and bra, even the thermal underwear. When she'd opened the magic clothes chest (that's what she was calling it) and held them out, she'd been a little wary about just how close a match they were (not kidding; the bra was even her preferred style, and if you knew anything about bras, there were at least close to a thousand shapes, styles, and whatnot). Anyway, she'd decided right then and there it was best to believe Grandma had done the shopping. Not Durlan.

Certainly not James.

She'd immediately slapped *that* thought away—James rooting around in her underwear drawer back in Grandma's rickety-old house, gray eyes contemplating each and every article with the utmost seriousness, memorizing each little detail, including the size of her bra's cups—yep, totally not going there.

She put the clothes on instead, and realized she'd been right.

A perfect fit.

Perfect to keep her cozy and alive in the middle of this winter... a winter taking place a year's time in the future.

Because of her.

She needed answers from Durlan, and she had a pretty good guess he was about as stubborn as her and wouldn't say squat until she'd done as he'd asked. Besides, her tummy was getting ready to revolt and twist inside out with all the growling and gnawing it was doing. The amazingly glorious smell of garlic and salted beef was really starting to take over the small cabin.

So, she ate.

And ate some more.

Finally, Kate scraped the insides of the wooden bowl with a wooden spoon, her third or maybe it was her fourth helping of the absolute-best, broth-like meat stew she'd ever had in her life, by the time Durlan finally got back.

The cabin door banged opened and a swirl of ice and snow howled inside.

Kate yelped and nearly dropped the empty bowl on her lap.

Durlan's heavy boots pounded on the wooden floor, dropping snow like he was shedding it as he swung inside, then slammed the door with a force even as the wind tried to fight him, to resist being shut out. Like it was alive or something. He succeeded though, of which she'd had no doubt.

Bits of snow had grown little ice sculptures along his beard. And his long hair, which was now flattened underneath his fur-lined cap, had their own orchestra going on, complete with an ice composer and his wand-like stick.

Really, it was pretty impressive. He hadn't been gone that long.

Was the storm really that bad?

Durlan's face was a bright red, making his eye-patch seem like a black hole right there on his face. For a moment, it didn't even look like he was wearing it... but no, as soon as she had the thought, it was there again, complete with the scar slicing out from underneath it.

The fire's heat seemed to blast him, and almost instantly melted away the snow.

Now, she wasn't a snow kinda gal herself. The cold and certainly nature had never been her thing (or her mom's), but she had a feeling that wasn't exactly normal.

But then, what in her world was normal these days, anyway.

Kate wiped her mouth with her sleeve, a very nice, thick, wool sweater. It wasn't one of her better habits, using her clothes as a napkin, but it wasn't exactly like there were any lying about, either. Besides, this was a sturdy sweater. She might actually have a chance at surviving Elsa's ice-winter out there.

"You mean Aila's," Durlan said.

"Wait? What—you *can* read minds."

He didn't answer her.

Figured.

Durlan tossed off his hat instead. "Good to see you've refreshed and joined us back among the living. It was not time for you to ride with the Valkyries just yet."

She pointed her spoon at him. "That makes no sense."

"And neither does giving such great powers to a young girl, barely a slip of a woman, really. Untrained, completely inept in all knowledge of who she is, where she comes from, with not only the ability to cross worlds but apparently bend back time."

Kate blinked at him, surprised. That sounded like the longest thing he'd ever said to her. And pretty darn comprehensive, too. She certainly didn't disagree with him.

"About losing time," Kate said, "losing a year, I didn't mean to—"

"Regardless, you did it. Even for a second, child, it has great consequences. All it takes is a small amount, one glimpse back into that past..."

He waved his arm towards the door. "To create this."

The wind, which even now, pushed and pulled against the heavy door. Rattling right there on its hinges, like if the wind just pushed hard enough, blew hard enough, it would succeed, and this little haven of warmth would be done for.

It was really, really hard not to slouch into those warm fur blankets and hide.

He was mad at her. Still.

Rightly so, it seemed.

Durlan took two steps forward and slapped two bodies—yes bodies —of white hares on the small table beside his rocker. Now she understood quite well what meat was, where it came from (and not from the magical grocery store where it was handed to you on a white cardboard platter and wrapped in plastic) but still seeing Durlan's catch up close and personal like this...

Well, honestly, she didn't have those kinds of luxuries anymore. She was lucky to be alive. And food, nourishment, was required.

Hell, if the ice storm out there was what he'd been alluding to, especially being a magic one... caused by Aila?... well, she should be impressed he'd managed to catch *anything*.

"I don't think I can help you." She nodded at the rabbits. "With that. I mean, with what to do with them or cook or—"

"I know. And that, is my point."

Durlan yanked off his coat and tossed it at the peg hanging out the wall. She got the clear sense that, this time, he wasn't mad at her exactly, but that she (like always) was the cause of his anger.

It really was a feeling she was used to, with Grandma and now with Durlan. Guess those two really did have a lot in common.

Kate got up, filled her bowl with more of that wonderful meat stew, and handed it to him.

"I don't know how to skin a rabbit. Or clean one. Or cook one. But I'd like to think my mom taught me something."

"Kindness?" He asked. "Manners?"

"I don't actually know."

Not yet, anyway.

He shrugged, as if her apology meant nothing more than those frozen puddles of snowflakes fallen about by his boots, but he accepted the bowl.

And then, finally, he told her a story. A couple of stories, in fact.

But first and foremost, the story about her missing year.

CHAPTER SIX

Kate sat on the bed again, legs crossed, knees pressed to her chest. The warmth of the fur blankets, of the fire still roaring steadily behind her, did nothing to push away the chill working its way through her heart.

And the shiver that wouldn't stop.

Durlan sat on his rocking chair, spooning himself the garlic beef stew in between words, but she barely noticed the pauses. Barely noticed how the howling wind outside had increased in intensity, as if it had a say in this story, a voice all its own, and it was angry about him sharing it with her.

A bit of stew dribbled down Durlan's lips and got captured in that gray, bushy beard of his. He didn't bother to wipe. Didn't bother much with anything, except eating and speaking and staring, staring down at her with that single eye of his.

It didn't leave her, not for a second. The swirl of colors flicked from green to purple to gray.

She deserved it, too.

Durlan had told her what happened, from the moment Kate had left her camp. Grandma. James. Aila. How it was Aila who'd first sensed Eolis nearby and took off running to find her former husband,

and to get Kate before he did. (Kate already knew this part of the story; Eolis himself had told her Aila was coming... and she'd chosen to go with him anyway. Course, that was before the whole messing-with-time-thing.)

But Grandma hadn't gone with Aila, which in itself was curious. Why hadn't her trigger-happy, shotgun-loving Grandma gone in guns-a-blazin'? Literally. Instead, she'd stayed put. So had James.

And when Aila came back without Kate, Aila had demanded of James to ask the trees to find Kate (she'd hadn't a clue he could even do this).

But... but of course he would tell his mom, regardless of the connection he and Kate shared, regardless of how he felt about her, how his own elven soul felt about Kátheryn, he would have told his mom. He believed in her. Trusted in her.

And this whole time, she'd been using him. That had been part of the reason she wanted to return, to leave the glade and find them, so she could help.

Of course, only making things worse.

Her heart twisted at the thought. Torn, almost in half.

"James told her, his mom," Kate whispered. "Didn't he?"

"No. He didn't."

"But, how? She's—"

"A right powerful bitch and 'bout as kind a one as his mother. Now. I believe I'm the one tellin' this story, here."

Kate shut her mouth, listened, and found out just how much she'd screwed up.

The Gathering, the whole entire, stupid reason Kate was even out here in the middle of nowhere, hiking and camping and everything that went with it (like no flushing toilets or shampoo). All that serious, important, elf-descendant business, , didn't actually happen. That's right. This Gathering who were *supposed* to decide what to do about Kate and her magic (and Kátheryn to boot) didn't happen.

Kate's mouth dropped open. "You're kidding me? All this, and no one showed up?"

"That's right. No one showed up."

Kate knew, thanks to Kátheryn and the Memory, that Aila's whole plan had been for Kate to take some test (whatever it was) and fail. All so Kate would go running and crying back to the one person who would accept her:

Her dad.

Yep, that's right. Evil magi dad, who kinda had tried to kidnap her (and failed), and who had a serious grudge against all things elvish.

Clearly, Aila didn't know Kate in the slightest. As if she could ever forgive him, let alone *trust* him after that.

She snorted. "No Gathering. No me failing her stupid test. I'll bet Aila was furious."

Durlan's eyes flashed purple. He glared at her. "You. Tell. Me."

As if to emphasize his point, which probably *was* the point, the wind gave a really hard slam against that door. The rusty handle rattled. Snow slipped in under the frame and shot towards her, pelting from where she sat with those fur blankets. And the wind didn't stop either. Not howling or blowing. It came on so hard, so fierce, it shook the whole cabin.

The small chimney, where the smoke from the fire was safely escaping from the wind, came roaring back down. The flames went crazy...

Until Durlan glared at it with his one good eye.

Suddenly, both flames and wind behaved.

Then, he glared at her.

"Uh... right," she said. "The storm. This winter. That's... that's Aila? But, how? I mean how does this all fit in, the storm, the missing year..."

The golden larch leaves frozen in time.

Kate shuddered. No, she hadn't forgotten about those.

She pulled the fur blankets tighter around herself, but it did nothing to warm the sudden, deep chill she felt.

"You kept saying this was my fault," she said. "That I went back in time. I saw the Memory of the forest, and then... then this happened."

"Child, you don't even know what the hell you did, what you broke in the first place. Can't know what to fix until you understand what you broke."

"Well, then tell me, because that is the one thing no one wants to do around here."

"No. They sure don't." Durlan watched her for a bit. "You saw a Memory. You understand how that happened?"

"Kátheryn... she showed me how to connect with the forest. It was the forest memory I saw and—"

"Before *that*, you were walking the veil."

"I—wait, what? I was in the veil?"

"It might not have seemed that way, seeing as how your focus was on the forest, but believe me, girl, you were there. You were walking the veil, stumbling through it more like. The veil, you see, ain't just a place separating the worlds, it's a place separating time." He pointed at her. "Which you went and busted right on through."

"And... and I caused... this?"

He nodded. "By going back, even as a shadow of yourself, because that's what you *were*. You were a shadow of the forest as you watched that piece of the story unfold. And in that moment, you were there. Beside Aila. Your father. You were there."

"And then... after I saw the memory. I was back in Kátheryn's glade. With Eolis."

Durlan's face went red at Eolis's name. His eye deepening to a really, really dark green. Clearly, Durlan wasn't a fan.

"And in her glade, in that moment, after your magic had created this bubble, this opening, you were outside of our time. For a whole year, you did not exist in this time."

She had a hard time breathing. And if she'd decided to stay, even if for one night... oh god... how much time would she have lost? Grandma? James?

Her chest tightened, hurt at the very thought.

"A lot's happened in that year," Durlan went on, relentless. "A lot that can never be mended or changed. And that includes Aila and her wrath."

"I see that."

Except, she didn't. Not really.

And Durlan held nothing back. The mind-reader that he was (clearly, even if he wouldn't admit it) knew damn well how to hit a message home and to never, ever do something this stupid and ridiculous again.

He told her the rest, or at least as much as he was ever going to tell her.

How the Gathering didn't just show up, they'd *disappeared*. Each and every one of the elf-descendants, at least the ones considered important enough to show up—gone. Missing. Like they'd vanished straight from the forest. And those who hadn't been willing to make the journey, well, they were gone as well. Some while driving (leaving their cars to run off the road into some poor tree), others while drinking coffee and reading the newspaper.

"Grandma?" She dug her fingers into her crossed legs.

Durlan shook his head. "She survived the disappearance."

She let out a heavy, shuddering breath... but Durlan wasn't done. Oh, no. When he wanted to pound a message in, he pounded it.

Just like that stupid wind outside.

The magi? They were back in force.

They were the humans who, when the elves had first come into this world a thousand years ago, bringing all the magic with them, were changed. Altered. Or maybe some part of them that had always been open to magic finally had the chance to make that shift. They were touched, gifted. The elven magic went and opened up a uniqueness all its own. Human, magical gifts with their own abilities, ones completely and totally different than the elves. And their elf-descendants.

Magi, though, were purely human, and it hadn't taken them long to hate on the elves. Hated how they'd entered this world and begun to think of themselves as gods, who saw humans as lesser and beneath them. Kate had never known much about this part of their history. Grandma hadn't told her much, or really, hadn't even much time to tell her (before Kate started getting into trouble... like running into her dad and nearly breaking time).

Durlan got up and spooned more stew into the bowl, then handed it back to her.

She didn't protest and took it. He didn't speak again until it was empty.

And even more, she was feeling her strength return (and had a feeling that was going to be real important, real soon). Not Kátheryn, though. Her candlelight, that flame, was still dim, and clearly still hiding from Durlan.

So be it. They both probably deserved the silent treatment right now.

"The magi returned," Durlan finally said. "They overwhelmed all of Alfeim, my forest. And Lighthome, your mother and grandmother's home. It's not like you remembered. Never will be again. Not after them."

"But I don't understand. How... how did this happen? How did my going back, seeing one Memory... cause, cause all this?"

Durlan's mouth thinned into a tight line. So small it seemed to disappear right amongst all the other scars mappin' his face.

"Which is why the gift should never have come to you. No mortal. No human. Not even elves. A mistake, clearly."

He seemed to be talking to himself, if only for a moment, but then his gaze, his single eye, turned back on Kate.

"You created a ripple, Kate Silver. When you went back, saw what you had no business seein', you opened a gateway. In a way, you allowed for this change to happen. All Severi ever needed was an opening. Your dad, the cunning bastard he is, had been waiting for just that moment."

Durlan leaned towards her, his tall frame covering the short distance between rocker and bed, and even sitting down her towered over her.

"He'd been waitin' this whole time for you. To screw up. You... and Aila."

From the Memory, and what Eolis had told Kate after, it had been clear that Aila had had plans of her own. She'd never planned on handing Kate over to her dad or risking James if she failed Severi. What she'd wanted though, as far as Kate could tell, was her own magic. The real powerful stuff, not what was left behind when the elves up and vanished.

Aila had wanted the elves to return.

Her dad, again, from what Kate could tell, wanted the elves returned too—but just so he could finally destroy them.

Kate swallowed. She didn't understand all the details, how Severi, her dad, had taken that opportunity, that opening she'd made to change things... and so much else, too. The magi returning. The elf-descendants, missing. Aila, too, having gone all ice queen. She had too many questions, but for now all that mattered was one.

One question.

What the heck was she going to do about it?

She felt it, that choice within her. It didn't come from the dull flame that was Kátheryn or that part of her that was her heritage. Instead, it was all her, and it was her choice on how to move forward.

To hide, or...

Do something about it.

She didn't know where her family was—and Grandma *and* James were her family now. So was that little town of Lighthome, Montana, with its cracked pavement, no stop signs or stoplights (why need it when the population was like four). And while still not accepting of her (being able to cross magical veils separating worlds, and apparently time, too, was admittedly a bit difficult to accept—*and* not be terrified of), it had been her home.

For two months, sure, but longer than any other place, in all the ways that mattered most.

And... and Eagle, too, her spirit guide. Had he been taken as well, punishment and cost for using the magic? She had the sense that yes, it was. And if she wanted to atone, if she wanted to right this world, she'd have to earn him back again.

Then, there was James to consider. James, who she couldn't sense or feel. Did he know she'd returned? Did he... did he sense that she was back?

From the first moment she'd come to Lighthome, James had known exactly where she was. Sensed her, like always, and in a way she'd always sensed him.

Not anymore.

Kate stood and faced Durlan. There really wasn't a choice, not really. Not for her.

"Okay," she said. "I want to fix this. I *will* fix this. Just... just tell me what I need to do."

"Can't."

She blinked. "What? After all that, that *lecture,* and you can't even tell me what I need to do?"

And this was exactly why she kept getting into these situations. No one would ever tell her the whole stupid story, or gee, consequences would be nice!

Durlan pulled out his pipe from some hidden pocket of his fur-shirt thing.

"Your problem. You fix it. Those are the rules."

"Says who?"

Kate felt more than saw the blue lightning spark around her. She crossed her arms. "Right. Doesn't matter who."

Durlan pulled out some dark rock from the same hidden pocket, with a mere flick of his fingertips (along with a very definitive display of blue lightning). He took a deep breath, then puffed out the sweet, tangy smoke back.... right at her.

Kate's eyes watered, and she tried hard not to cough. Or gag.

"Course... " Durlan puffed again. "You can start by dealin' with him."

He pointed to the door with his pipe, smoke trailin' behind him like a reaching finger. The metal latch twisted up and the door burst open. Snow and ice and tumbling wind flew right into that small cabin.

Along, with James.

CHAPTER SEVEN

J*ames.*

Kate couldn't move. Not the way her heart pounded, ready to leap right on out her chest. And breathing? Forget it. Totally beyond her.

So, she just stood there, loose hair blowing out behind her like a mooning idiot or some damsel in need of saving, her socked feet glued to that dusty, wooden floor. Her heart raced like she'd been waiting for this moment, this chance to reunite for an age (and not the few hours it had actually been... well, for her, anyway).

Except... it... it was him.

... right?

The thin, lanky boy she'd known (though to be fair, very, very close to man) now wore a thick, heavy coat, and it was pressed tightly against his back from the force of that wind. The sheer rage. Snow and ice battered against him, knocking him down as he turned and scrambled to close the door. Ice crystals hung from his equally heavy, fur-lined hat, which, even if she could see his hair, would probably just look the color of snow. Then there were the dark goggles he wore, and the cloth pulled up that protected his face and nose.

Just by looking at him, she didn't *know* exactly if it was James.

Except, that she did.

Felt it... felt it through and through, from the candlelight that was Kátheryn, the way it flared to life as if it had never dimmed, not even for a moment. Forget using the time magic. Forget the consequences and all that.

In this moment, Kátheryn was a raging bonfire all her own.

Plus, Kate felt it in herself. The connection. This *was* James. Her friend, her, well, not anything more, not yet but there it was, somehow still burning bright and strong and this time, this time it was all her. No influence by Kátheryn and her desperately wanting the elven soul mate living within James.

Kate wanted to run across that short cabin, knock over Durlan and his stupid, puffing pipe—who was just *sitting* there rocking. That's right, sitting there puffing away and not helping James who got knocked down, yet again, as he tried to slam that ridiculous door closed.

James was on his knees, struggling to close the door, pushing with his whole body. His thick gloves made that last bit, closing the latch, just about impossible.

—The wind shoved it open again. Nearly knocked James right in the nose.

Or where his nose would be if he weren't wearing the mask.

"What is wrong with you?" she snapped at Durlan.

He puffed a circle of smoke at her and grinned. "Not my fight."

She swore at him, knocking aside his book as she scrambled forward. Thank god she was skinny enough to squeeze between Durlan's mile-long knees and the wall, which even now shook with the rage of Aila's winter storm, like the woman wanted to reach on through the wood and pull Kate out the other side.

Kate smacked into that door with every ounce of force and energy she had—and her shoulder instantly numbed.

Icy cold pierced into her as if the thermal sweater was as useless as her T-shirt had been. Not a normal storm, not a normal winter.

Not in the least.

But together, she and James pushed. He never once looked at her, never acknowledged her, and that didn't matter. They were a little busy right now. But she'd be lying if she didn't feel the burning light within her, from her and Kátheryn, and the singing, humming word that kept vibrating through her.

Especially as her shoulder, numb even as it was, touched his.

James.

Right now, keeping the storm and its rage out was all that mattered. Until her completely frozen, totally numb hands (boy, she'd hoped to never feel *that* again), got that metal latch closed and the door, finally, stopped trying to jump off its hinges.

Thank *god*.

Breathing heavy, grinning from ear to ear, her poor hair once again going in about every direction possible. Snowflakes and ice sprouting out in every which way. It looked like she'd traded the leaves and sticks from hiking for the ice and snow of winter.

Kate turned to James, desperately wanting to fling her arms around his neck, to hug him for all she was worth, tell him how *sorry* she was—

He wasn't looking at her.

Wasn't acknowledging her or her presence at all.

His attention was totally and completely on Durlan.

"Thanks for the help." James swiped down his mask. Tossed it at her bed. "You could have warned me."

Durlan shrugged. "She's your mother."

"Yeah. Don't I know."

James yanked off his hat, goggles, tossed those at the bed, too. Snow covered every inch of him, like it was as much a part of him as the new lines etched along his face. They hadn't been there before. They were hard lines, not the joyful kind around the mouth from smiles and laughter. As if he hadn't felt a moment of joy since she'd seen him last.

For her, a few hours ago.

For him, a year.

But there was no doubt that a year had indeed passed.

James's blond hair was longer, too. The bottom curls brushed the back of his neck now, compared to sticking up straight in just about every direction. And yet, even with most of it tied back, it was still springing out like it had a mind all its own. But, as different as he was, it was James who stood there. Right there, right beside her.

Kate wanted to reach out, to fully close that short distance, this half-foot separating them. Brush her numb fingers along his shoulder, touch his longer hair, as if such a simple gesture would give her all the answers she needed. Could fill in those gaps that now, clearly, existed. He was not the boy she'd left, but a man. Hard with harder lines, an angry, defiant stance without an ounce of fear towards Durlan.

Durlan, who even Kátheryn hid from.

And yet... the urge to touch James, to close that distance, was still so strong. Part of her prayed that such an act, as simple as it was, would just... erase everything that had happened, and they could go back to the way things were.

Silly, yes, but still a hope she felt flickering, bright and true, as clearly as she felt Kátheryn's.

But she didn't touch him, didn't cross that short distance separating them.

Again, there was that feeling... a feeling that told her such a gesture, a connection, would not be welcome right now.

In fact, would be... resentful?

Kate dropped her hand instead, fingers somehow even more numb and cold than when the wind and snow were rushing into the small room.

Durlan gave another puff of his pipe. Blew the smoke right at her. "Bout time you started listenin' to your insides."

And, as if by Durlan acknowledging her presence, James finally turned and faced her.

She'd been right about those lines, now etched hard and deep into his face. They were not put there by laughter, but by sorrow and loss. The kind of loss that sucked everything kind and good right out of the room, right out of you. Stole everything you loved and held dear, even hope.

"What... what happened to you?" she whispered.

What *had* happened in that year she'd been gone... to... to turn him into this?

James's eyes narrowed.

At least they were the same gray eyes she remembered, though harder and colder. But like before, they were still just as piercing and perceptive as always. The same eyes that never allowed her to hide. Not from her fears, not from the truth.

Never, from him.

Or from the connection they'd always shared. Like a golden string of light and ribbons, always tying them together. How she could close her eyes and hide anywhere in the dark, in Alfeim Forest, or even when she found herself walking the veil, that misty place between worlds, when she could see him. Feel him.

Not anymore.

That connection, was gone.

Just... just gone.

"James."

His name just about tore from her. Pure sorrow, one she felt as clear as the distance now separating them.

A distance he did not attempt to close. Instead, he crossed his arms and glared at her.

"Took you long enough."

CHAPTER EIGHT

Snow drifted down from the heavy gray jacket James wore and littered the ground separating them, melting into the floorboards. Becoming a thin layer of mud from the dust and tracks that Durlan had already brought in.

Outside, the wind continued to howl, to beat at the shuttered door. Trying its best to enter, to intervene.

Kate almost wished it would because, in that single moment, she'd been working side-by-side with James and he hadn't cared who she was. They'd shared a purpose, a common goal, as simple as it was.

Close the door.

Now... now she doubted there was anything at all between them. Except... except maybe her desperate need to see things right again.

Even if... even if they never could be.

Because there was no question about it. This was not the boy she'd left in the woods.

The boy who she'd felt herself falling for, but she'd been too scared, too afraid, to trust in her own feelings. Could you blame her? With Kátheryn right there, coming closer to the surface every day? Kate hadn't known if what she'd been feeling was truly hers, or if it'd been Kátheryn.

And James had understood. More than understood, in fact. He'd promised to stay friends and to wait, as long as it took... but then, that was before Aila had intervened, and the next thing Kate knew, from breaking camp one morning and hiking to the next site, he'd suddenly stopped talking to her. Like he'd thrown this giant ravine of distance in between them and he would not cross it.

Wouldn't talk with her, or even look at her.

James, the person she could always rely on, and he'd suddenly refused to come near her.

Was it any wonder why she'd gone with Eolis in the first place? That she'd—stupidly and willingly—trusted in Kátheryn, a long-gone elf who *clearly* had an agenda all her own, who'd been the cause of this whole, stupid mess to begin with?

She had to try, though.

"James, I—I'm sorry. I didn't know. I didn't know about the time magic or the memory, Kátheryn, she didn't tell—"

"What else is new?" James didn't wait for her to answer. He turned to Durlan. "I did as you asked. My part of the bargain is done."

Durlan pulled the pipe out of his mouth. His mouth curved upward, and his single eye glinted purple.

"As you can see," Durlan gestured to Kate, "I fulfilled my part."

"She came through on her own," James countered.

"Fat lot of good that' a done you. Her being dead and all."

James nodded. "Fair enough."

Kate stepped between them. "Wait? What? What part? What are you talking about?"

"Nothing that concerns you," James said. "It's not like you were here when the deal was made."

"That wasn't my fault—"

"Wasn't it? I thought going back in time and seeing a memory that *neither* of you had no business seeing was pretty cut and dry. But then with you, it never is. Rules just never applied. Even now."

Kate stumbled back a step. At his anger, his coldness.

What had happened to him? What happened to the boy who loved riding his horse bareback? Who always had a ready smile for her and that perfect, mischievous spark, daring her to be different?

To be herself?

Durlan stood and his rocker scraped against the floorboards so hard she couldn't hear the wind. At least for a moment.

"Seein' as how you two kids got yourselves all this catchin' up to do, if you don't mind..."

Durlan made a shooing motion towards the door.

James straightened.

Kate went white. "Wait? We're supposed to go outside? In *that*?"

"I told you," Durlan said. "That part ain't my fight. I did what I came to do. Now, I'll leave you both to it."

James was the first to react.

"Fine. As if I expected more." He crossed to the bed, snatched up the goggles and mask he'd thrown down. Turned and glared at Durlan. "But then, that's about as much help as the elves got before they disappeared."

Durlan's single eye began changing colors. From purple to green, then to another, so fast she could barely keep up, until finally... settling on black.

And then, came the lightning. It was the same blue as before, and it started zipping and snapping about the suddenly very small, very cramped cabin. The lightning, so close and powerful, it was already making her hair stand up on end.

"I would be very careful of what you speak." Durlan's voice rumbled, so deep and full it felt like thunder. "You were not there that day. Your Aevar does not remember."

A living thunder, that's what he was. Right inside their cabin.

James didn't react. Not to the thunder. Not to the very clear growing threat of this man who was clearly *other*. The big shadow stretching up and outwards from Durlan, like it was going to swallow the whole cabin, was a pretty good tell.

And there was James, not moving a damn inch, or for that matter, backing down. The idiot.

"How do you know what Aevar does and does not remember?" James asked.

"Because I was there when his soul left this earth."

"A soul," Durlan said, "that I demanded ride with me, but who refused."

Again, it felt like the whole foundation of the cabin rumbled with him. Kate reached out and steadied herself on the wall. Ice immediately leached into her body, and she yanked her hand away.

Durlan took a step closer to James, who looked so small, so tiny, even as he stood there with his back so straight, his hands balled into fists. He didn't shrink away or shiver. Just... stood his ground. So angry, so cold. Not caring at all that Durlan's shadow now engulfed the cabin and was reaching... reaching straight for him.

The fire from earlier, the one that had warmed her and heated her delicious stew of meat and garlic, suddenly snuffed out. No red embers remembered, eating away at the wood, slow and methodical like. Not even a lingering trail of sparks. Nothing. Not even smoke.

Just, just gone.

Durlan's mouth did not move, but in her mind, Kate, very clearly, heard him say:

"No one refuses me."

James tilted his head, and for a moment, Kate saw the other him, the other soul living beside James's. The elf, whose name she finally knew.

Aevar.

Aevar had become like a shadow image laying on top of the James she knew, or at least the James she used to know. Gone was the boy with his springy blond hair and the warm down coat. Instead, his long gray hair was tied back by a thin leather string. But the tie did little as strands were blown back by Durlan's presence. Aevar stood in his brilliant silver mail, and she could almost see, almost imagine that yes... this, this was exactly how Aevar looked when he last faced Durlan, with his feet planted in moist, rolling earth. Earth that was practically living and sparking with magic and the thundering voice of Durlan.

Except... no. That couldn't be right because the last time Durlan and Aevar met... he'd been dying.

And just like that, as if the thought opened up some third eye of hers or whatever, she began to see the faintest traces of something...

flowing from his brilliant, shining armor... except no... not as shiny now, but covered in mud and dirt.

Streaked, very clearly, with blood.

Kate sucked in a breath. Was she using time magic? But... but she hadn't done anything. This was just her normal (okay, nothing was really normal about her life was it?) sight that sometimes got triggered. She didn't know what caused it or why it happened, though always, always when James was around.

And... like that day with Aila, on their very first day of hiking when she'd cornered Kate and had pretty much, in no uncertain terms, said to stay the hell away from her son. Eagle had shown Kate something else, another image of a shriveled woman, hunched and bowed, a woman who'd been afraid of *Kate*. And of James. Of what they could do together.

Eagle had helped her see a deeper truth. Was that what Kate was seeing now? Or was she screwing things up again, and when she opened the front door it'd be like Death Valley out there?

God, she hoped not. She *really* hated the heat.

But just as quickly as the image appeared, it faded.

Well, not completely, cause Aevar was still standing there, all superimposed like over James. Except for the eyes. Those were James's, as well as Aevar's.

Gray and piercing, and again, never once looked at her. Not a glance. Not even a flick in her direction.

Which was ridiculous. To a long-lost elf soul, separated by some crazy-ass time (like a thousand years) and he's so pissed that he can't even look at her (or, Kátheryn)?

Apparently so. Cause Aevar just stood there, completely indifferent to her. He cared more about the stupid sword on his belt, the one he very deliberately put his hand (which, as far as she was concerned, was just drawing a line in the stupid stand).

Oh, it was also a glowing *silver* sword. Chances were this meant the points from said line were worth double (it being a magical sword and all).

"I refused the hunt," Aevar said. "I refused to ride."

"You did," Durlan agreed. "For her."

"The reason matters not."

"But doesn't it?" Durlan grinned. "Promises made. Promises kept. Both of you made them."

Durlan's grin turned into full-on menace. Whatever human form he'd taken before, or mirage of himself, or illusion, whatever it was— totally gone. Now there stood a very strong, feral... *being*.

No, seriously.

This dude was starting to look messed-up scary. Imagine pointed, sharp teeth and an inherent, deep promise of really, really bad things to come—*that's* who Durlan reminded her of.

And James, or Aevar, didn't care at all.

Nope. Seriously. Like they didn't seem to give a shit about, you know, *living*.

And regardless of how mad he (they?) were at her, she was not super keen on him dying. Or herself, for that matter. Also, she was really, really starting to get some massive shivers. And her premoni- tions? Her feeling and little-warning-o-meter?

Yeah. It was freakin' out big time.

Big time.

Kate shook her head. Her blond hair fell about her shoulders, and she felt the wetness from melting snow drip down the back of her collar. She felt it, but in a distant way, enough to remind her that she was still alive, and she was standing in a cabin with two magical beings (and a seriously, scary-looking shadow) ready to go berserk. Not to mention the winter storm outside doing her damnedest to get in.

"Uh... James?"

But James didn't care that she'd spoken, or if he did, she sure as hell couldn't tell. It was like he'd gone completely numb inside, just as cold as Aila's raging winter outside this cabin. It was like, standing there, staring down Other-Durlan, James didn't care one whit about that power raging off this man, err... being, who seemed really, really ticked that some boy, a human one at that (with a healthy dose of elf thrown in), dared defy him.

It was really not the best way to go on living.

Especially when Durlan's shadow was about ready to eat James. Or Aevar, glowing sword or not.

Kate felt the candlelight within her. Kátheryn, for sure, but some of Kate, too. Her own magic, her own light. It was still there... her spirit guide, maybe? Eagle, somehow, from wherever he'd been banished, reaching for her?

She didn't know, and honestly, there was no time to think. Certainly no time to think of a better (or smarter) plan. Only time enough to act.

And that's what she did.

Neither Durlan or James gave a damn that she was there, that she had anything to say. So, Kate did the stupidest thing she could possibly think of, but the one that would get her the most attention real quick, without all this screwing around.

She stepped between them...

And walked right into magic.

CHAPTER NINE

Kate didn't know who Durlan *really* was, this gray-bearded mountain man who preferred to wrap himself in furs and hides over anything you'd go and buy at an REI store or something. Including his boots. Like his boots had never once seen the inside of a factory (certainly not a third-world one), but were hand-stitched with some thick-ass thread.

Probably specially ordered, too, and made by some guy who went to work uphill, in the snow, both ways.

Those were some heavy-duty snow-boots, and Durlan had planted them on that dust and snow-fixed floor, grounding himself, getting into a good stance like he was ready to rumble. Seriously, she could almost see a stupid line drawn out in sand (err... melted snow) on the cabin's floor.

And James didn't seem to mind about that line, or care. At all. In the slightest. Or that he was about the size of dust speck or an ant compared to Durlan.

Nope, he just stood there, straight as his pushing high five feet, not quite six, could. Fists clenched at his sides, tendons all sticking out on his neck and forehead. Gray eyes glaring right up at the big ol' mountain man who was about to spew smoke out his ears.

Or maybe that was the lingering smoke from Durlan's pipe.

Ugh. Even now her eyes watered at the smoky, tangy smell. And she seriously thought about opening the door... if she could actually get it closed again.

Who knew, maybe *that* would dissolve a bit of this stupid male tension. Maybe.

She'd inadvertently caused this when she'd used Kátheryn's time magic. She'd caused these two men to come together, in just this way. And whatever had happened to James during that missing—whatever it was that made his soul turn to ice—*that*, that was straight-up on her.

Like hell was she going to stand by and not doing anything about it.

She would fix her mistakes. And keeping James from dying by this crazy powerful being? Well, that seemed as good as any place to start.

Of course, she should have started by *not* standing right there in the line-of-fire. But she needed their attention...

Not that that seemed to have made much of a difference. Neither man acknowledged she was, you know, *standing* there. Right between them. That if she got squashed in the process of them battling it out over the line in the wet cabin, oh well.

That wasn't going to happen.

Besides, they hadn't gone and got all concerned about her disappearing, trying to get her out of Kátheryn's glade for a year if they really didn't care if she ended up dead.

It was a bet she was willing to take.

Mostly, because she wasn't alone.

Kate held her hands up higher, one towards Durlan, one towards James.

"You seriously need to stop. Now."

Their hard gazes looked at her and she glared. Right back. First at James, then at Durlan.

Honestly, she probably looked a sight. Wearing her now-wet wool socks on that suddenly freezing floor. Hair blowing this way and that, bits of snow and water from when she and James had wrestled the door closed, flinging every which way as Durlan turned his thunder-force on her.

Not to mention the scary shadow that had snuffed out all the light in the room.

Except for hers.

Which, he tried to do.

Oh, yeah, did she feel that whammy. How he turned his single eye on her, so deep and dark you could almost see yourself falling into that blackness. Falling and falling, with no idea of which way was up or down, or if it really mattered anymore.

Kate felt his magic, whatever was his power. He... pulled at her consciousness, her soul. Like this *was* his power, the ability to suck all life on in and spit it back out again (...if he wanted, she imagined, for good measure, he probably didn't do much actual spitting).

She had a pretty good idea in that moment that Durlan wasn't some 'being' at all.

Try god.

Maybe even with a big 'G' kinda god.

That was getting overly technical, and right now she was doing her best to keep upright, keep breathing, and dear lord above, keep James doing the same.

He'd seriously been trying to a pick a fight with this guy?

Course, said a whole lot about her seeing as she was the one standing right in the middle of it. Yes, well, too late to back out, even if she wanted to.

She didn't.

James, or Aevar as he appeared at this moment, long, gray-haired elf in the shining armor and glowing sword, yeah *that* guy, well, he finally saw her. Yep, her. The person who held the soul of his supposed true love.

And it only took her stepping into mortal (and very possibly immortal) danger, but hey, great, the guy finally saw her, noticed that she existed after being one for like, a thousand years.

Aevar's eyes went wide with shock. "Kátheryn."

Her name, like a whisper. Full of wonder and... pain.

Then the moment passed, and his gray eyes shuttered so tight, so suddenly. Like this glimpse of emotion, that for once wasn't cold-white anger, wasn't actually real. Hadn't actually happened. That perhaps, she'd imagined the whole thing.

If not for the deep, sorrowful ache in Kate's chest. So sudden, so fierce, she nearly collapsed at the knees at its force. A feeling that came not from her own self, but from Kátheryn.

Clearly this was not the love reunion she'd been expecting.

"What the hell are you doing?"

This time it was James's voice. Not Aevar's.

To be fair, she thought, this wasn't the reunion she'd been expecting either.

At least, though James sounded incredibly pissed at her, in a small way, it was very much like the James she remembered. The James she'd known for those two short, wonderful, amazing months.

Kate couldn't help the small smile.

Sure, she was standing between two magical beings ready to duke it out, but it was all worth it. Just to know that he was still in there. The James who got super exasperated when she went and did really stupid things, like... well, like this, stepping in front of super-pissed off god and what-not.

Yes. Well, about that...

The wooden boards along the cabin floor shook. Several popped up right at the nails, and one cracked right in half. Splinters flew into the air. Cut into her pants. Some, into her palm. All show and anger meant to frighten her off, of course.

Kate stayed put. (Though, she did wince when the splinter sliced right into her hand, drawing blood and everything, cause man did that one *really* hurt.)

"Really? Was that necessary?" she asked. "That *hurt*."

"Better to bleed than lose your soul," Durlan rumbled.

The lightning came again, closer this time like it was trying to sizzle her skin. She was also pretty sure her hair *was* standing straight up like Doc Brown from *Back to the Future*.

Dear lord, was the guy scary.

"You have no place here, small one," Durlan said.

"Kate." This time, from James. "Stay out of this."

He was reaching for her—

And she pulled away.

"No. I am *not* going away." She pointed at Durlan, well, as much as she could with her throbbing, blood-dripping hand. "*You* told me to fix my mistakes. Fix what I broke. That includes this."

The lightning got closer, the jerk.

She liked her hair just fine the way it was, thanks very much.

"Step away, small one."

"No."

Durlan did not respond back to her. But then, he didn't really much need words when his magic did the responding just fine.

His presence *pulled* at her again. No more taunting her or joking. This was serious mode and he was seriously turning on the magical, soul-sucking whammy.

Apparently, he really didn't care a whole lot if she up and died. Good to know.

The darkness of his eye, his shadow, both swallowed the whole room with her and James in it. Pulled them right on in. She reached out to do something logical like grabbing the wall or the bed post, you know, something to keep her in the present and in the suddenly, very dark, freezing cabin.

Her fingers brushed against the rough wood of the wall, and then they passed right through it. She fell and fell into darkness, and as she did, she felt something like sorrow ripping into her. The opposite of life, something worse than death. Oblivion. Complete non-existence, that sorta thing. And he just kept right on going, ripping away at her, taking big ol' bites into who she was, her conscious. Like he was trying to untether her soul from her body one bite at a time.

It'd be so easy to give in, to simply stop fighting.

To let go.

Because that's what all those sorrowful, soothing voices were whispering to her in that falling darkness. Sure, she couldn't see anything, but she could hear just fine, and it sounded like she wasn't alone in here either.

Urging her to give in, to let go. Wouldn't it just be so much better if she did? So much happier, too?

Here she was, fighting to save a man who wanted nothing to do with her, who *hated* her, not because she made a mistake, but because she'd trusted someone else. Trusted Kátheryn and Eolis. Trusted someone that wasn't him.

He'd never forgive her, the voices whispered.

They continued to pull at her. Pluck at her. And she noticed how her light was getting a little bit dimmer. One rosy strand of flame sizzling out of existence, one small spark at a time.

And then another voice was asking her, well, why didn't she just let go? Stop fighting?

Actually, it sounded an awful lot like her mother, which had Kate stirring.

This sense in her itching... that... wait, that wasn't right. Her mom had left her here...

But the voice was quite soothing. Quite... well, motherly, really. And she was pretty persistent to at least be heard. How Kate had never been meant for this life, living as some kind of 'elven' descendant. After all, there was a reason they'd run and hid her whole life. Why the truth had been hidden from her for so long.

All to keep her safe. That's what mothers did.

And what she'd done, the voice continued to whisper as another spark of gold-rose blinked out, was out of love.

All Kate had to do was let go and it'd never be a problem again. She would be safe. Perhaps, then, she even could be the normal girl, the normal teenager she'd always wanted, always *dreamed* of being.

Simply... let go...

But... she couldn't. Something else, or someone else, was calling her name, reaching for her cold, numb hand. Fingers... brushing against hers? She couldn't tell because she couldn't quite feel.

Then there was the peeling thunder overhead, or no, was that her heart? Beating?

Sounding... a bit too fast, maybe. Hard to tell as she was simply swimming in all this blackness.

Another voice came, this one cold and hurtful. Disdainful.

Her father.

She barely knew him, but she'd know his voice anywhere. That charming melody, one created for deception and temptation, and now with his usual crisp clarity that allowed nothing to hide or be hidden, told her she wouldn't amount to anything. That she hadn't the skills or the fortitude to succeed. That even if her mother had allowed her to grow up in Lighthome, surrounded by her heritage, by the forest, she'd fail.

She was too weak.

Too... human.

Her father, with his sweet soothing voice, did not stop. Oh no. It was like he knew exactly what to say to cut right to her heart.

Another spark of gold-rosy flames slipped away.

Kate deserved what happened next, and what had happened to everyone she cared about. She was a foolish, foolish girl. One who never learned, who never paid attention, who never cared about consequences.

All this, all that had happened, was her fault.

Only hers.

Kate felt the flame within her fall away. More sparks this time, like a cascading mountain finally breaking free and sliding into a lake by the force of the earthquake shaking it apart at its foundation.

Her flame flickering faster. Growing duller, dimmer.

Nearly, gone...

CHAPTER TEN

As her little candlelight, that dimming flame, somehow tried its best to hold on, to keep on lighting against all the darkness, the cold that was filling her nose, pressing against her lungs, making it harder and harder to breathe...

Her father's voice turned harsh. Angry. There was no shaking the surety in his voice, the confidence, especially as he told her that all this was her fault.

Her *light* had been too weak.

And... well... maybe he *was* right. Cause look at her candlelight. It was barely there, barely a glowing red-orange on that last bit of a wick. So maybe that meant he was right about everything else, too, what had happened with time and with Grandma and James...

James...

Another voice, a softer, kinder one, whispered to her. A voice that caused her stomach to swirl and the butterflies that sometimes lived there to tremble and flutter. A voice that always made her smile.

He was calling her name. Telling her to come back.

Kate turned in that swimming darkness. Squinted her eyes to see him, to see any sign that she wasn't actually alone. Nothing. But... she reached anyway, reached out with her slow, numb hands as if he was right there just, just a foot from her if she just gave it her all...

And didn't give in.

Her father shoved into her. His presence. His force and magic. He pressed, harder. Colder. And the darkness, somehow growing even blacker, denser. A few more sparks of light sizzled away. Kept pressing, kept closing in on her and her suddenly very dim little candlelight and the last of its light, its color.

Golden and rosy.

But... was that all it was?

This time the thought came from her not from any of the other floating voices. Didn't she glimpse another kind of light there? Silver... and blue... maybe green?

Kate felt her awareness blink awake. Felt herself turning closer to her own light, almost like she held it out in her hands, and peered at it. Warmed her hands there, her fingers, and for a moment, her flame brightened.

She saw, quite clearly, there *was* another kind of light and color in the flame.

She wasn't alone, after all.

Her light, it was still there. Still, hers.

And then she thought... well, why did she care what her father thought or what *he* said about her?

She didn't know him. Didn't want to know him. He was not her father, not her dad, even if the guy had passed on his genes. He was a right jerk and could go screw himself for all she cared. *He* was the real reason this mess started. He'd taken advantage of her mistake, knew damn well she'd make one (or a lot). He was the real reason she was in this shit now.

Not her.

The candlelight within her brightened a tad more. And yes, there was indeed another color right there, though it kept winking in and out of view like it wasn't quite yet in place.

Like she didn't quite... believe in it.

Yes, this flame was Kátheryn, though not as warm and strong and secure as she'd been in the glade, before they'd gone and messed up time. But Kátheryn's light, her golden-rosy hue, it *was* getting stronger. Not just this dim little flame, one barely holding onto that last tip of a candle's wick, but—

Kate's, too.

That's right, she had her own light.

Kate felt rather than saw a hand reach out and gently touch her shoulder.

Encouraging. Welcoming.

She didn't pay much attention to it. Right now her attention was on herself and her own light.

She'd never seen it before. Maybe she never had to because she'd always had Eagle beside her. Eagle who'd guided her, who'd been her gateway to magic, to her heritage. Maybe... maybe this was just another form, one that had been inside her the entire time.

She didn't know, doubted anyone would give her a clear answer even if she asked (that was sorta the running theme around here). But no question about it, she had her own light, and hers was a silvery flame with the tiniest flashes of aqua blue and green slipping round and round. Almost like a living spiral. Almost like life itself.

Kate breathed in.

The air sparked with Durlan's lightning and the thickening smell of smoke and pine and hickory, wherever the heck those scents were now coming from. Right now, she didn't care.

Instead, she focused inwards.

Went into herself and then just dove... down, down, then down further still. Kept going, kept going until she saw in her mind's eye those two flames as they flickered side-by-side. Both were just small, little things. Like the kind of flame that only cast a dull orange glow about a small room. Not nearly bright enough to read by, certainly not enough to cast out darkness. Certainly not the kind of darkness ready to snuff out your soul.

And yet... it would be enough. More than enough.

She was enough.

And the moment she thought that, truly *believed* it... the flames changed. They slowly came together. Blending. Still two flames, still mostly separate but, in some areas, becoming one. Fitting together in a way that felt natural, that felt right. Both colors, both unique shades—no, not shades or colors, but... *souls*.

A piece here, another... there. Each sliding into place. Some places were whole and right, other areas still missing. Like a puzzle that wasn't finished yet, but... it didn't need to be either.

Not for this moment.

And just like that, her light brightened. Became fuller. Spread out into the darkness until she saw a room. A room with that narrow bed, with heaps of furs and blankets thrown on top. A room with that rocking chair, still rocking, but not from the raging winter storm outside those thick, wooden walls. Oh, no. It was rocking cause of the storm taking place right here on the inside.

The more she focused on her light, on how bright *she* was, the more the darkness pulled back.

There was the fire, poor thing that had been snuffed out, and not a trail of smoke lingering over it. If her tummy wasn't full with all that delicious stew she'd never have guessed it'd been used recently. Or this century.

There, too, was the snow and dust, that mixing, wet slosh on the now uneven, and in some places ripped-up floorboards. There was also the black ice that lined the walls and ceiling, like it'd come straight from the dark void itself and decided to up and leave its mark. But the ice wasn't growing, wasn't lengthening into super sharp icicles, so that was plus. In fact, as she watched, water—well, black water—dripped down... staining those ripped up boards the same black.

Best to stay away from whatever magical residue *that* was.

Kate edged away from the little puddles, even as the darkness pulled back further still until she actually saw herself again, standing there in her wet wool socks, arms outstretched between James and the being who called himself Durlan.

Finally, the darkness snapped back to where it had come from in the first place.

Durlan.

Durlan, whose eye was no longer black, and was now slowly changing into that dull green again. James, she noticed, was watching her, too.

Definitely James. Not Aevar and his shining mail or glowing sword. Just James. And... she couldn't even begin to interpret the look he gave her. Still hard and cold, but also... something else.

Relief, maybe?

Or maybe that was just her projecting cause she was feeling pretty darn relieved, herself.

But for a moment, she felt that butterfly flutter in stomach. Almost like hope. Like... had that really been *his* voice calling out to her? When she'd been lost in all that hopeless darkness, had it been *his* hand reaching for her, trying to bring her back? Like maybe, just maybe, he still cared.... even after everything that had happened this past year.

Then the moment was gone.

His gray eyes hardened, and she practically felt him, felt his light, pulling away from her. Like he wanted nothing at all to do with her.

Kate let him.

Really, breathing was pretty darn hard at the moment, and if he wanted to be that way, well, she had her own issues. Like, *damn*, did her chest hurt. It was almost like she really *had* been breathing in nothing but ice and cold. Probably the same black shit dripping all over the place and staining all those nice, comfy furs. But really, whatever Durlan had done, whatever void he'd created and sucked them into, it was worse than when she'd been standing in Aila's raging winter, wearing nothing but her ripped jeans and T-shirt, stumbling through that snow with those frozen, golden larch leaves.

Much, much worse.

Kate slowly lowered her hands.

"Like... I was saying. You didn't really go through all that trouble—just to kill us both off."

Durlan's brows arched up. "Seemed like a good idea at the time. I do have a bit of a temper."

"No. Kidding."

Kate took another heaving breath, warmth again filtering into her body. It also helped when the fire suddenly lit all by itself. Red and orange flames, cracking logs, along with a flurry of angry sparks at having been snuffed out in the first place.

She didn't even blink at that one.

Seriously, not the least surprised considering what she'd just been through, what with walking into winter and the whole void-sucking-darkness thing. And to think, she'd only been back a day.

"I think," Kate said, "we've pretty much determined that I can't do this alone. So, thank you. For not killing him."

Actually, they shouldn't leave her alone for a second, since that was about how quick her life went to hell.

"You so sure 'bout that?" Durlan asked.

"What?"

"I think... you don' a mighty good job of it, right there."

He tilted his head at her, gray beard standing up every which way, probably from the same thunder wind that had hers in about a thousand knots right now. He nodded right where her heart was, as if he could *see* her two souls...

No, that wasn't right. The single flame within her.

And this time... a little bit brighter than the candlelight it had been before, even back in the glade.

Stronger. Brighter.

And filled with magic.

Kátheryn's, and... *hers*.

Kate blinked. Her mouth dropped into a big 'O' shape and she forgot all about standing there in her wet socks or how truly terrible she looked with her hair going every which way.

Durlan drew out his pipe again—she had no idea from where. Maybe some inner pocket, maybe from out of thin air (at this point, she wasn't about to discount *anything*, certainly not when it came to this man). He lit it again, though this time being very clear he was using his fancy blue lightning magic to do it. He took a long, long inhale, before puffing it out.

That damn smoky smell again.

At least he puffed it in James's direction for once... even though she was still pretty much standing between them. She rectified that right quick, as her eyes watered and her throat got scratchy.

"And you, James Skye?" Durlan asked. "I reckon I finished my end of the deal."

James, who hadn't moved from his spot, like his feet were glued into the wooden floor panels... at least the ones that weren't ripped up and strewn about the place in chunky-sized pieces. James's hard gaze met Kate's, but then he turned and nodded to Durlan.

"A deal's a deal," James said. "She's back."

"And mine?" Durlan asked.

"Like I told you. I got what you asked for. You'll know where to find it."

Durlan nodded back.

"Wait a minute here." Kate waved her hands about the room, the *ice* suddenly lining the inside of the cabin's walls. Black freakin' ice above all things. "Are you telling me all *that* was just an act? All part of your... your stupid deal?"

"Nope," Durlan said. "I was plannin' on killing you both, right there."

Kate felt herself go pale.

Well, at least he was honest. Bonus points for that.

"Certainly felt real." James tugged at his heavy jacket, right above his heart.

"Because it was," Durlan said. "I do not play."

"Neither do I."

"Then you best be dealin' with your own issues if you wish to live long. Not too long, though. Reckon that life's not callin' for you, either of you, but certainly long enough to deal with your mother. Long enough to clean up this mess."

Durlan said this last to Kate.

She certainly didn't blame him. It *was* her fault.

Again.

James stopped tugging on his jacket, like he was convinced that yes, his heart was still there. "I'll deal with her."

Then he glanced at Kate. Real quick, as if he couldn't bear the thought of actually looking at her.

"I honestly didn't think you could do it," he said. "Even you."

Durlan's chest rumbled. It almost sounded like a laugh.

"I told you I'd bring her back. I did. All of her."

And there they went again, talking like she wasn't standing there herself. Like she didn't have a say in all this. Or a choice.

Well, she did, damn it.

Especially when James was shaking his head, acting like an arrogant jerk.

"Honestly, there wasn't much to bring back. Not of use. She hadn't found her magic. Or even believed it was there."

Okay. That was enough. Especially after she'd just gone and done all that, all that light stuff and, you know, saved his life or something, ungrateful jerk.

"Excuse me." Kate slapped her hands on her hips. "I *am* here you know. And I already told you, that it wasn't my—"

"Fault," James said. "We know. It never is. Too bad we couldn't wait around for a a whole *year* while you got it together. Especially *you* were the one who went and screwed up the veil in the first place."

Her mouth clicked shut.

It felt like someone had thrown a bucket of freezing cold winter water all down the front of her shirt. James had never... he'd never said anything like *that* to her before. Was this... was this how he'd always felt?

Stunned, hurt, she could only stand there and, and listen.

And James was only too happy to keep going.

"You created the opening for *your* dad. You went back in time and left us, left me, even after you *knew* she'd just woken up."

"How, how long have you felt this way?"

She barely got the words out. Her throat, suddenly so dry.

And honestly, she couldn't quite follow... was James talking to Kate right now, or was Aevar to Kátheryn? Or hell, were both men one and the same and simply just pissed off at her because she'd disappeared for a year, with no clue at all if she'd ever come back?

Her head spun.

This, this right here was why she'd taken a step back from all those swirling butterfly feelings. Too confusing. Too hard to tell what was her and what was Kátheryn.

And now, make that doubly hard seeing as how their two flames were kinda one.

"Or maybe," Durlan puffed out another disgusting ring of smoke, "that is also the point. For both of you."

"Will you stop reading my mind?" Kate demanded.

Durlan merely grinned. No more sharp teeth, though, so that was something. Actually, they were quite yellow and looked like they needed a good brushing... no way in hell was *she* telling him that.

Durlan sank back into his chair and rested a mile-long leg against his knee. "As I told you both, my bargain is concluded. And with that, I leave the rest of this mess, for you."

For a moment the blue lightning was back, but this time sparking in his eye like he was having a right fun thunderstorm right there.

"A mess you *will* clean up."

His eye, which saw everything. Future. Past. And every which way in between, every time fragment and line breaking off and shattering from the main one they were walking on.

An all-seeing eye.

From an all-seeing man.

"Holy shit," Kate whispered. "You're Odin."

James snorted. "I can't believe it took you this long to figure it out."

She wanted to smack him.

Durlan's grin just widened, as if he'd seen all of it before, future and past, and still, it pleased him.

Now *that* worried her.

"Promises," he reminded them. "Both are still owed to me, even those who've been long gone from this world, and who've returned."

"Wait a minute," Kate said. "Kátheryn made a promise to you?"

Durlan, of course, didn't answer.

"Now," he said instead. "Go clean up your mess."

He waved his pipe, with that smoke trailing every which way and making her eyes turn red. Then suddenly the fire, the warm bed with all those warm fur blankets, the cabin, all of it, disappeared.

And they found themselves standing in the middle of the frozen, Montana wilderness.

CHAPTER ELEVEN

The cabin was gone.

Kate hadn't seen the outside when she'd first arrived, dying from the elements as she'd been, but she imagined it'd have been a presence out here, in the middle of this forest and all. The only man-made piece of dwelling for miles. Its little chimney poking out the top, stones cobbled together any which way they'd go. A trail of smoke, too, maybe even carrying that last lingering scent of that oh-so-amazing garlic and meat stew.

All that, just gone.

No indentation along the snow, not flattened or squashed like there'd been a building, you know, standing there. Not even tracks from when James must have trudged through the snow just to get inside.

There was... nothing.

Kate turned around in the flat, untouched snow, taking in everything.

Just a small clearing, maybe a little meadow during the spring or summer, when the ground was covered with grass and pine needles and cones. Now, it was just a blanket of snow. Some small tracks ran off in one direction, maybe a winter bird, maybe an arctic fox (they all looked the same to her).

Surrounding her from all sides were pine trees and larches that had so much snow hanging off their limbs and branches they were sagging down by the weight. Some even brushed along that snowy forest floor while their tops looked quite similar to pointed white Santa hats.

At least the trees that weren't just frozen over, and there were plenty of those.

Needles and branches looking like they'd been reaching out for help, begging, doing everything they could to escape some icy blast other than picking up their big, thick roots and simply running. Which they couldn't do. As far as she knew, anyway. These days, every-thing was a possibility.

So... frozen trees, snow tracks left by some animal, no cabin.

It really wasn't a huge shock, all things considered.

Nor was the cold, actually. Like maybe the dual flames inside Kate, one doing its gold-rosy bit and the other silvery one with its mix of aqua and green, did a little internal heating of their own. Which was nice.

It probably helped, too, that sending her back out into a winter storm in wet socks would have defeated Odin's purpose of saving her from the elements in the first place.

That's right.

Odin.

Kate didn't know a whole lot about Norse mythology, or Odin, just the bits she's picked up in school (when paying attention), also, too, what Grandma had let drop about Yggdrasil, the World Tree (who also happened to be a good friend of Kate's, at least in this realm, anyway). She didn't quite know all the implications of what it meant, having Odin save her and kick her magic, or whatever she had, into gear like that (or why he bothered with her at all, for that matter). She certainly hadn't a clue what he meant about those promises he'd been talking about—other than, you know, her screwing with time.

He'd been pretty pissed about that.

Kate shivered at just the thought.

Yeah, pretty mad. Certainly not something she wanted to repeat.

Temperamental god that he was, though, he had weird sense of humor. Durlan had been kind enough (though she seriously doubted 'kind' was the appropriate word here) to make sure Kate was properly clothed for her second venture into Alfeim during winter. She might be standing right in the middle of a snow field, snow reaching her hips, but hey, this time she was wearing super warm wooly socks (very much dry, thank you), this heavy-ass deep blue coat with white fur lining the hood, and snow-proof pants.

That's right, no more cotton, water-absorbing jeans.

And gloves. Couldn't forget the gloves.

Kate lifted her hands and wiggled her fingers. She could even *feel* her fingers, too!

So, yeah, that was a pretty good start, even though the wind was still bitingly cold, especially the way it swept right past those frozen trees, like those wind ninjas were gaining speed just to bowl her over. As if its whole purpose was to cause her teeth to chatter. At least the wind didn't have the same force as earlier when it was slamming into the cabin, trying to rip the door right off its hinges.

No, definitely not the same. The intensity, the intention of the wind right now... it was definitely different.

And yet, even still, Kate had this sense that something—or someone—*was* there. Watching, maybe. Like it wasn't just the natural elements as God had meant them to be, but... more.

The wind gave another shrilling blow, picking up loose clumps of snow and flinging them at her. Not forceful, but oh so cold it cut right through her jacket and wool sweater and thermal underwear combined.

The wind tugged at her hair, and a few strands snapped right at her eyes.

Definitely deliberate.

Kate felt it. Felt that lingering intention, like a cold, cruel smile curling up.

James stood nearby, or near enough, like he didn't want to come within two feet of her if he could help it. He had his goggles on, though they were dangling around his neck now, along with that cloth he'd been using for a mask. A dusting of snow already covered his shoulders (courtesy of said-wind) and quite a few flurries had caught in his hair, too...

Which again was its own reminder.

His longer hair, which thanks to the sun breaking through those heavy, gray clouds above, she could see better now. And yes, it really was longer. And... maybe slightly darker, too? Like he hadn't seen as much sun, so his hair didn't have its usual summer gold.

Another reminder that time had passed.

Not that his glare wasn't reminder enough.

First at her, then at the wind as it continued to snap and pull between them, as if wanting them to come closer. Which was odd in itself. If it *was* Aila behind this storm, this winter, the last thing she'd ever wanted (at least a year ago) was for Kate and James to be together. *That* had been a huge part of the fight that had sent Kate stomping off into the woods and running right into Eolis.

Yeah, Eolis. James's dad.

About that...

Kate took a deep breath. The cold air helped her head stay clear and kept her own frustrations under control.

"Okay," she said. "So, are we going to talk about this?"

"Talk about what?"

"You're mad at me."

"What gave you that clue?"

The icy glare was back in his eyes. Jesus, it really *did* look like he was just as iced over as those trees, his was just on the inside. Hidden, though not to her. James was also making sure she knew it, too. He clearly had a whole lot he wanted to say, and she probably deserved every bit of it.

Again, another breath. Trying her very best for patience and understanding.

"Durlan," she said. "I mean Odin. He didn't tell me a whole lot. Just about how I opened a gateway for my dad to work some pretty powerful magic. He told me about the Gathering, the members who disappeared, but not much else. Not the details, anyway. So, I don't... I don't know what happened."

Her throat closed. The words stuck there.

"I don't know," she said, "exactly, how I hurt you."

"You left."

"I didn't know that would happen."

"No. Of course, you wouldn't. That would require insight. That would require understanding who you are, your heritage. And for once, accepting it."

He... wasn't wrong, of course.

Kate had wanted answers. Hell, that's why she'd stayed in Montana in the first place. But acceptance? No. She'd only grudgingly accepted who she was right after all the bad things (and her screw-ups) happened. She'd been doing her best to keep her head buried in the sand, even when the magic started flying. And part of her, even as she had learned, as she got get better, still kept on denying.

At least until Odin and his void of soul-eating darkness. Now, however...

Kate's hand reached up, touched the spot near her heart and her dual flames.

James pulled up his head and pushed it so low she could barely see his eyes. He glanced up at the sun, looked around once, as if trying to get his bearing or turn on his inner map or something. But whatever it was, he clearly knew where to go (or she seriously hoped he did), because he started pushing his way through the heavy snow.

He also didn't wait for her. Or even tell her to follow.

Nope, just left.

Clearly, he was not interested in having this conversation now. Or maybe ever.

But she needed to. She couldn't just keep stumbling along like this, making one mistake after another. She needed to understand. It was the only way she *could* learn.

"James, just... just please wait."

"Why? It's not like you waited for me."

She stumbled after him. "I want to make this right. I want to fix it."

"Some things can't be fixed."

He didn't look at her as he said it, but oh boy, she had a pretty darn good idea what he meant. Not exactly, cause that would require him, you know, *talking* with her. Something he clearly had zero interest in doing.

But obviously she'd done something. Broken something. Her leaving, her being away, had caused something to happen to him. And whatever it was, she and she alone, was the cause of his coldness. A cold that didn't feel much different from the wind, even as it continued to tug at her blond hair, as the strands snapped and stung her cheeks.

It wasn't a far cry from saying it felt like the wind was laughing at her or chortling mercilessly.

"James! Can you please just slow down?"

Kate scrambled after him and nearly face planted when she found some fallen log her boot just happily caught for her. She dodged that one, got her balance, and then...

Nope, never mind. There was ice on that one. She was totally going down.

James spun.

So quick. Fluid, graceful. A single movement.

One moment he was furious and stomping away. The next, he was there, holding her upright. His right arm encircling hers. Their breaths, so close they were almost touching.

And she felt his touch straight through her jacket... but not the searing warmth as before. The kind of touch that had heated her through and through. That made her whole face go red and her toes want to just curl up.

His touch was nothing like that now.

It was completely ice.

An icy cold that shot straight through her, went right past her heart and headed straight for her two flickering flames. Freezing everything it touched, bearing down on those flames with a single, determined focus, one goal, one desire to freeze—

James immediately set her down. Let go.

Actually, he about flung her back into the snow. So sudden and unexpected, Kate nearly slipped on that frozen log again. This time, she managed to stay upright. Which was good because oh god was she cold.

So, so cold.

Her arm, right where he'd touched her—completely numb. Her teeth, chattering.

It was a feeling that felt way too similar to walking into this scary-ass winter frozen-land, when Durlan had picked her freezing self out of the snow.

"James?"

He wouldn't look at her.

Her teeth kept chattering, making it hard to talk. "Wha, what—"

"It's not safe to talk here."

He turned away.

She reached for him with the arm that wasn't icy and numb, and... and hesitated. She truly did. And that felt like the worst betrayal of all. This... this was James, after all. He'd been her friend and possibly, something more. How could she hesitate? Even if, even if there was that... that magic...

Kate rubbed her arm. The cold, still there. Not warming nearly fast enough even with all her layers and her special winter jacket. No mistake about it, it was definitely magic.

"Are you going to tell me why?" she asked.

"Maybe."

"About why it's not safe to talk? Or about the cold?"

James straightened. He glanced back at her, and yes, his gaze went right to her arm. Right to where he'd touched her.

"Like I said, some things can't be fixed." Again, he turned away from her. "And some things are just meant to be."

CHAPTER TWELVE

James set a hard pace. It was like he needed to keep moving, keep pushing forward. No snowbank seemed too deep or big for him, and he trudged on through, never once breaking a sweat.

Kate certainly was.

She'd never imagined you could get hot while in the middle of winter simply by moving your body on some snow hike, but wow was she hot. Strands of hair stuck to her forehead and cheeks, cheeks that she was pretty sure were bright red from the cold. Oh, and the lovely wind that decided to keep them company the whole way.

Hours, in fact.

Ugh, was she exhausted. So tired. Hungry, too.

James had a pack with all the essentials in it—nearly frozen trail mix and an equally hard bag of jerky that nearly broke her jaw in her attempt to eat it. He'd actually shared with her, which was surprising.

Of course, he'd been very careful to not touch her.

In fact, he'd been pretty careful to not stray within two feet of her. The second she started closing the distance, maybe so they could have a conversation, you know, fill her in all those little details about her missing year (and Grandma and Aila's deal with this winter wonderland), but the second she did, he backed away. So, no, she couldn't even get close to him. And the jerk knew, too, that she couldn't keep up with his grueling pace, so, well, she got to look at his ass the whole way.

It was a good ass, though. Nice to see that some things didn't change.

Actually, it wasn't until her legs were about to fall off, when the glints of golden sun snuck on through the clouds warning them that it was approaching evening, that she saw why.

James was sweating, but unlike her, his sweat froze on him. Little beads of water so small she'd have missed it if she'd been panting any harder. Or, if the sun hadn't decided in that moment to push through those gray clouds (growing heavier and more crowded by the minute) and she'd seen that little frozen glint of light off his skin.

She'd nearly dropped the bottle of water she'd just been chugging down.

"James! Your skin, it's—"

And, as if he had the same mind-reading ability as Odin, he swiped the bottle from her, stuffed it back into his pack, and stomped off.

All without touching her, of course.

"Are you kidding me?" she called after him. "You're not going to talk about this?"

No answer.

Figured.

But you know what? She was tired of this silent treatment. Tired of just following blindly and he still hadn't told her anything. Not what happened (*certainly* not to him) or Grandma, or even where the hell they were going. She was done playing nice and giving him his stupid space.

Kate ran after him, using the trail he'd already cut, flinging snow left and right for any in her way.

Damn it if she couldn't control her own swirling frustration. Nothing she ever did was good enough. Every time she tried, every time she learned a bit about herself, about her heritage or magic, she went and screwed up and got blamed for what happened. Never mind the fact that no one was actually willing to stand up and take responsibility *for not teaching her*.

No. It was all on her.

All her fault.

James, of course, didn't stop. In fact, he picked up the pace as if that could stop her.

Well, it didn't, and she was riled up enough where her elven talents kicked in and she *could* keep up with his ass.

Good-looking ass that it was.

"You know what?" Kate yelled at his back. "Yes. I've stumbled along ever since Mom dropped me off here, but I've been trying. I've done what everyone asked of me, most of the time with only half-answers or none at all. Gee, kinda like this. So, yes, I've made mistakes. What do you people think will happen when you never tell me anything?"

James froze. Back so freakin' straight, hands into giant-gloved fists. She might have even seen one of those frozen sweat beads sizzle off.

And she really didn't care.

She stomped right around until she stood in front of him, stood just a small foot away from him, and oh damn did he tense at that. He backed up a step and she followed.

"I hurt you," she said. "Something happened, I haven't a clue cause you won't tell me. You won't tell me about my grandma or about my dad and his evil empire of magi, and I'm getting seriously tired of everyone blaming *me* when you've been in this stupid, messed-up situation way before I came along. Like a *thousand* years."

He backed away from her. Again, careful to not touch her. "We're not talking about this now. We need to move."

She followed, right on his toes. Didn't care one whit if her boots brushed against his and she lost feeling. Well, that'd already happened to her once today and she'd survived it. It'd be worth a little numbness to finally get some answers.

"No," she said. "No, we *are* going to talk about this now because you clearly need to. You're pissed at me. I get that. But be pissed at Eolis, *your* dad, too—"

"He's not my dad."

"He used to be. And be mad at Kátheryn, too—you know, your Aevar's soulmate. Cause they both could have told me what was going to happen when I viewed that memory and they didn't. If I'd known, I wouldn't have."

James snorted. "Yeah. Same excuse you've been using for two months. Oh, no, excuse me. A *year*. Because that's how long it's been for me."

Again, he turned away from her. Shoving his way so fast through the snow he was making a wind tunnel of flurries and ice all his own. Kate didn't let up. No way was she letting him stomp away. No way was she letting him leave without telling her exactly what happened.

No more living in the dark. No more just blanket accepting the blame.

There was more than enough to go around this time; it wasn't just on her. Everyone, even her grandmother, had their own fair share here.

"You have no idea what I went through," Kate said. "You have no idea what happened, what I saw—"

"You went with Eolis."

"Of course, I did," Kate snapped back. "What was I supposed to do? Will you please just stop and talk to me."

Of course, he didn't. Fine then. She rushed in front of him, coming within a bare inch or two of his arms, his chest.

James wasn't expecting it, which was surprising. Even more surprising was how he stumbled, not graceful or fluid, like he'd suddenly lost connection to that part of himself...

Or maybe he was just so terrified to touch her that getting away was all that mattered.

He slipped on some hardened ice and nearly went down but recovered at the last moment.

She nearly forgot what she was saying, because James and slipping was not in her world view. Not even close, but no... this was her chance and she had this sense, maybe coming from her dual flames, that this was the only one she'd get.

James wasn't looking at her. In fact, she could see his battle, his refusal to acknowledge her right now.

Why was he so afraid? What didn't he want her to know?

Kate pushed aside her hair with her gloves, feeling the cold trail of snow and ice from the cloth. All around them, the forest had this mix of silence and noise. Quieter than it had ever been during the summer months, what with every bug imaginable out and chirping and biting, and yet it was a forest alive with many creatures. The soft calls of birds brave enough (and apparently warm enough) to survive the climate. The far-off trickling of water from some stream or river that hadn't yet fallen over. And she thought, maybe heard, the telltale scream of a great eagle as it circled high, high overhead.

The sound heartened her, brought the tiniest smile to her lips. Even now she wasn't alone. She was strong enough for this, strong enough to ask for the truth and accept it.

Kate took a deep breath of that freezing air and let it out in a puff of whiteness.

"James. What did you think would happen? What *could* I do? You and Grandma, you didn't believe in me anymore. You two, the people who always did even when I didn't believe in myself."

"It was complicated."

"No, no it wasn't. You were hoping this trip would awaken some elven part of me and it didn't. You were hoping the Gathering would see the real me, the elf-descendant me, so I could fulfill yours and Grandma's dreams and bring back the elves and all. Except I was still *me*. Stumbling me. Making-mistakes-like-crazy me. Can't even cross a stream without falling in. You pretty much told me the Gathering was going to rip out my soul."

"Kátheryn's soul, not yours—"

"Who, if you haven't noticed, *is* part of me. Kátheryn *is* a part of me."

His gray eyes finally looked up. Met hers.

"Aren't you even going to ask me what I saw?" Kate said. "What Kátheryn felt was so important to risk... all this?"

Kate waved her hand, gestured at all that snow. The heavy trees sagging from both snow and ice. The frozen sculptures. The frozen leaves. Pine needles. And... those golden larches.

They were the only color in this wintery world. A brilliant gold encased in ice. The leaves weren't large like a maple tree's, but smaller.

And all together, as they held onto the tree with its dark, almost black trunk, it looked like sunlight.

Sunlight hidden in winter.

Her heart ached at the sight, at something so very wrong. Something she desperately needed to fix. To change. And here, with James, was the start.

She *needed* to reach him, to get through to him...

Her, and Kátheryn.

Kate focused on her flames, the way they felt inside her, how they warmed her in a way she'd never felt before.

"James," she whispered.

She said this, as both Kate and as Kátheryn.

"It's true then," he said. "She's with you. She's awake."

"She is."

"And... you accepted her?"

A hard question because it was still so new, and she was still figuring it out.

"I did. I do," Kate finally said. "I trusted her enough to see the memory, and I'm trusting her now. She is a part of me, James."

James didn't answer.

Maybe he didn't want to know. Maybe he needed to keep on hurting, keep on believing whatever it was he believed had happened, because it was easier. Easier than the truth. Easier to keep holding onto all that coldness and ice than risk hurting even more.

A hurt he was entitled to carry.

The truth was Kátheryn *had* to have known what would happen. Eolis, too. And yet they'd pushed Kate to see the Memory anyway, to connect with Alfeim Forest, to trust in Kátheryn. They'd gone back in time, even for that small moment, that shadow in time...

And just maybe it hadn't been the memory itself that was important.

Kate touched her chest, felt the beating of her heart.

Just maybe...

She felt the warm burn of her two flames.

Maybe *this* was what they'd felt worth the risk. Her coming one step closer to accepting her heritage. And... of not being afraid of what that meant. Two souls coming together, but neither extinguished. Because she *was* still her. Still Kate. She hadn't disappeared like Aila had warned would happen. Aila, who had continuously used that fear, that threat to keep her and James apart, all because she'd been terrified of what would happen when their souls—his and hers, Kátheryn's, Aevar's—finally connected again.

Finally woke up.

Geez, four souls? Talk about a confusing mess.

James's eyes closed for a moment and he shuddered.

Kate had no idea what he was thinking, what moment in time he was reliving, though it was clearly one that she'd missed... missed because she was in the glade and out of time.

"I heard, you know." He opened his eyes. "From the trees. They told me Kátheryn had awakened. I was so... relieved."

Him and Aevar, too, she suspected.

His eyes were still cold, yes, but she couldn't help but wonder and hope... that maybe, there was something else there, too.

Something more.

Warmer and growing warmer by the smallest inches.

One drip of ice melting away. Then another.

James had been telling her all along, from the first moment they'd met in the grocery store, while she hid her and her weird pointed ears behind that Captain Crunch cereal box, that he'd known her his whole life. Had seen her in his dreams. Had always felt their connection, their souls, this golden string they shared attaching one to the other...

Could she see it if she tried? She had no idea. And maybe with Kátheryn, like this, she now could.

Or they could. Together.

Kate again touched her chest, felt her heart and imagined those two dual burning flames, the same but different. It felt like all she had to do was reach across this short distance between her and James. So close. If, if only he would listen, would trust in her again and she would take all that cold, all that ice he was living with and throw it as far as she could.

Or just melt it into a big snowman puddle with her flames.

Her... flames... her magic...

Kate almost saw his own flame reflected in his eyes, the barest flicker, like a candle just barely holding onto its wick as it fought to stay there, to keep burning, to keep bright... even as all that ice closed in around it. His flame, it looked like a goldish-red, and even though it was so dim, it was still so brilliant, so beautiful. Just this glimpse was enough to bring tears to her eyes.

This, *this* was James.

This was the James she'd always seen, had always known. Completely opposite of this coldness.

Kate reached for him. Her gloved hands crossing that distance. So short, just a bare inch, then smaller. A flurry of snow passed between them and then—

The moment was gone.

A black, heavy curtain fell so fast and so completely over his eyes at the same time as the wind picked up. It howled and screamed. Cut right through Kate's jacket, bringing the same snarling cold she'd felt tearing into that cabin.

She didn't care about the wind or the cold.

That, she could handle. That, she could deal with.

But James? How she could almost *see* the little bits of icicles growing in his eyes? Faster and faster. Like it was desperate to undo that tiny shred of warmth she'd seen, that she'd brought back.

Part of her, the sane, rational part, wanted to pull away. Actually, it had sirens blasting like crazy and shouting out every reason in the world why she should *stay away* from this man. It was pretty much a scroll of warnings and flashing lights, the same way they'd scroll across the bottom of your favorite news program.

It was a good thing that Kate ignored her critical voice. It was good, too, that she had such a high tolerance for doing stupid things— especially when they felt right.

Especially when she'd been so close to reaching him.

So, Kate did the stupid thing. Threw all caution literally into the wind and kissed him.

CHAPTER THIRTEEN

Kate had always been a fan of fairy tales, especially ones with true love and evil curses getting broken by true love's kiss. Not that she was expecting some instant, shimmering-white glow exploding off James. A light that blew right through the whole state of Montana and the evil winter was instantly gone (not that she thought winters in general were bad, just this one). Those poor, trapped larch trees with their golden leaves, suddenly free, and the ice holding James, gone forever.

That didn't happen, of course.

Again, no surprise.

Nor was it a surprise that Kate instantly lost feeling in her lips.

Losing feeling in her mouth, then her nose, and her whole face?

That was a surprise.

At least she could still keep breathing. Going numb was one thing. Freezing her face, like actually getting incased in ice like those larch trees and their sunlight-colored leaves, really not a good thing.

Kate immediately stepped away. Her gloved hand went to her lips. "Wha—?"

She went to touch it...

"No, don't!"

James, of course, touched her hand. There went the feeling in her hand. Arm, too. It'd probably been a reflex. He was still probably still just as shockingly surprised by the kiss. That she'd done it.

Or maybe the ice.

Their first kiss, too, by the way, and he froze her face off. This was so *not* the way she'd imagined her first kiss would go. She'd imagined fireworks and a coiling warmth, heat and fire, and all kinds of goodness rolling up and through her belly.

Not this.

And this was certainly *not* the same as earlier when he'd touched her arm. Which had eventually regained warmth, though it took an hour and some intense snow hiking. Course, there went feeling in that arm again, and it was spreading... down to her fingers, up to her shoulder, like the cold was a living thing all its own. It was like this magic, whatever it was, had grown. Had gotten worse, in just a few hours.

Or maybe... it had changed. Because of her.

Because she'd nearly gotten through to him, had nearly pushed past all that ice, and now it was mad. Now it really wanted to harm her. Destroy her.

Kinda like that super-pissed off wind which was now shoving and pushing so hard her hair snapped every which way. She barely kept herself upright and from falling right on top of James.

Which definitely seemed like the wind's intent.

And definitely would *not* be one of those cute, romantic scenes as seen on TV movies.

"Damn it to Odin, Kate." James stumbled away from her.

This was actually a good thing because she started pinwheeling forward, arms flailing, boots slipping on snow that had suddenly turned to ice right underneath her. And the wind just kept on going, throwing as much ice and snow at her as it could. Small sharp icicles biting into her face... which she couldn't feel, really, but like going to the dentist, she still felt the impact of those tiny, numb pings.

"What were you thinking?" James yelled at her. "I'm sorry. I forgot. You don't think. You *never* think. And here I thought screwing with time would have changed you."

Yes, he was mad. Yes, he was yelling. And sure, she might be Numb

Face right now, but he *was* concerned. In fact, she felt his fear... almost like it came searing down along their golden ribbon.

She blinked at the thought. Instinct telling her if she just reached out, maybe just the tiniest, tiniest tug, and she could touch—

James about stumbled another four feet away. "Are you seriously not listening to me? Do you have any idea what would happen if you touched that?"

"No!"

Well, she tried to yell. Hard to say squat with that wind roaring as it was. Or hear, for that matter.

Kate shoved her hair away, enough that she might actually see James through all that snapping blond. "How *can* I know when you won't tell me? I'm trying to break the spell."

"You can't break it! You're the one who created it."

She stood there, frozen just like those larch trees. "No. No, I didn't."

"You might as well have."

James stayed right where he was. The wind kept on howling, kept on flinging ice that bounced off their jackets, snow that splattered and then stung her eyes.

Neither of them moved.

"Tell me." Kate's voice shook.

"I don't know how." He didn't turn away though, didn't run from her. "You think this winter is just that, winter? You think it started because of some date on the calendar, some month that signals all nature to just change and start getting cold?"

"I imagine it's a bit more complicated—"

"Except *this* winter started the minute you left. The minute you opened that gateway for the magi and your dad, for the dark magic they worked. Trapped my..."

He didn't say his mother's name.

"She's the winter queen and she's cold and furious. At everyone. At life. You. Especially you. And it's been going on for a year."

"A... a year?" Kate asked around numb lips.

How was that even possible? And was it *everywhere*? Every place across the globe? Because then, how could anyone still be alive? Or, or maybe they weren't? Maybe she'd done something worse than she'd ever thought possible—

"No," James said, as if reading her mind. "Just here. Just our world. Alfeim Forest. Lighthome."

"But that still doesn't make sense. What about Glacier?" It was, after all, like right next door. "That's still here, right? All the tourists. My mom. It's still part of our world."

He shook his head. Snow stuck to his eyebrows.

"Not anymore. We've been stuck, right here, right in the middle of this winter. We can't get out, no one can get in, not that there's many left to try, thanks to the magi. But no one even knows to try to *get* in. They just can't see it."

"My mom—"

"What about your mom?" James shot back. "Why do you care about her? You think she's tried to reach you? You think I haven't tried to reach her, to get some help? Any kind of help?"

He wasn't wrong, not exactly. Kate and her mom hadn't left on the best of terms, what after her whole lying and deception for like, the total sum of Kate's seventeen years of life. But still... she was her mom.

Kate breathed in all that icy air. At least it was just this area that was affected. At least the rest of the world hadn't turned to ice.

Just here. Just Alfeim Forest.

And, and James.

"So, what about you?" Kate asked. "What happened to you?"

She pitched her voice as loud as she could. Her lips, still numb, which made the words feel odd, like they weren't really hers anymore.

"I'm her son. She's the winter queen." James lifted his arms, the heavy bulk of his jacket. "You can see the result for yourself."

Kate wondered if he even needed them anymore, the jacket, the gloves. Maybe he'd survived just fine in jeans and a T-shirt, and she had this little niggling feeling that he could.

He just chose not to. Chose to be as normal as possible.

Even if he wasn't anymore.

Oh boy, did she know all about *that*.

"I don't... I don't understand. Does your, does this happen with everyone?"

Kate waved in his direction, and at... well... at his lips.

His gray eyes held hers. "Yes, but not like this."

She was kinda hoping he didn't mean he'd kissed other girls, since... well, since she'd been gone.

"What do you mean?" she asked.

He still didn't look away, like he needed her to understand just how important this was, and that it was really not something she could just blow off or ignore.

"That..." James lifted his hand, touched his mouth. "That only happened when you tried to... break the spell. It's worse now, the magic. It's stronger. Because of..."

Of her kissing him.

So much for true love being the most powerful magic of all. Of course, she didn't know if that's what they had. Or ever could have. They'd never really gotten the chance to know.

But Kate had a feeling there was more to the story, more to this ice magic that was living inside James, than he was telling. No more stumbling around in the dark, though. She needed to know.

"James," she said. "If you want me to listen, you need to tell me. Everything. It's not just because of your mom. It's not just because I kissed you."

Which had failed pretty spectacularly, but hey, at least she'd tried.

She felt the truth in that, like it was humming right down that small, faint gold ribbon that connected them. She didn't try to reach for it, though. Instead, she was just grateful that she could still feel it at all.

That it was still even there.

James took a deep breath. Let it out. His breath didn't puff out cold like hers. Like he had no warmth, or very little, for this winter cold to even steal. And again, as if reading her thoughts, he looked away, almost like it hurt too much.

Oh, how she wanted to just reach across that suddenly huge distance, to hold his hands and comfort him, tell him it was going to be okay. He'd always been able to do that for her. It wasn't fair that she couldn't do the same.

"The spell," he said, "your dad's spell, all it needed was an opening.

I told you, you were the one who created this, and I didn't lie. You left, Kate. You left me. I felt the very moment when you disappeared from this time. I *felt* you, and then all of a sudden you were gone."

Through their golden ribbon, that's how.

James looked right at her. She saw so much pain shining right through the ice encasing his eyes, and she knew that it would have been easy for her dad's spell to grab him. She'd been the cause of that hurt, that pain.

"I'm sorry." Which was a really lame response. If only she could go back and change things, if only she'd been given different choices in the first place. "I didn't have a choice. Your mother, she—"

"Don't speak her name."

Kate shook her head. Let her hair keep on snapping at her, though she didn't feel it through the numbness.

"No, it's my turn now. You don't know what happened. You don't know what I saw. James. I saw *her*. She was in the Memory. She went and made a deal with my dad. All along, she'd planned on just handing me over to him so he could open the veil between worlds, so he could go find the elves and destroy them. Aila, she's been—"

James was suddenly there, suddenly beside her. His glove pressed against her still numb, freezing lips.

"Don't," he hissed. "Don't say her name."

He glanced down, saw that he was again touching her, and swore.

But it was too late. Both for his touch, which brought with it just not numbness but an ice so cold it easily ate its way into her system. Like when you touched a searing hot pan and even when you pulled away yelping it was too late. That pain, the hot, was already burning its way through your skin and it wasn't going to stop until it was good and ready. Except now, it was freezing, freezing ice.

Hungry and desperate. For her fires, the dual flames of Kate and Kátheryn. Their sizzling and sparks of magic.

And she knew in that moment, that was its whole purpose, this spell. To eat away at Kate. To freeze over both her souls.

She'd always been stronger beside James, of course. The first thing she'd do when she walked back into time, this winter scary-land, was try and reunite with James. Her own magic, awakening. Her two souls, finally, coming together. Of course, there'd be a trap to stop all that.

A trap that was living inside James, who'd known it the whole time and tried to keep his distance.

Course, he hadn't said anything until now. You know, when it was too late and all, which *really* made her want to scream, numb freezing lips and all. She'd give that howling wind a run for its money.

Was it a spell placed on James by Aila? Or by her dad? And really, did it matter?

Her teeth were already clattering. Her breath becoming heavier, like she was having a hard time filling up her lungs with that super-charged, cold air. As if the simple act of lifting her chest and exhaling was growing harder.

Each one becoming a struggle.

Which really, really wasn't good.

"James," she tried to say.

His gray eyes widened, as if realizing how dangerous the situation had suddenly gotten. Not just out for walk in the winter woods. Sure, a winter being controlled by a magical, crazy bitch, but it hadn't been exactly life threatening unless Kate had gone and fallen down a crevasse or something (she still wouldn't put it past her). Now, though, now was a whole different story.

For a brief moment, though, she thought she saw James's own flame shine through.

She felt panic, the flickering edges of it. Air was beyond important. It was life and if she couldn't—

No. No, she would *not* give in. She would be okay. She would keep breathing, and her lungs... well, they didn't have much of a choice in the matter because she *was* her own stupid force of nature and not just some ice spell trying to attack her.

Of course, that wasn't all, though. Certainly not the worst part.

The worst was that the wind, had indeed, heard her. When she'd gone off, yakking away like words meant nothing and names weren't powerful. Like talking about James's mom out loud and all.

Because of course, the wind and his mother answered.

CHAPTER FOURTEEN

Unsurprisingly, the wind became a force.

Kate had thought it was bad before, when it had slapped her hair about and tried to shove her right on top of James and trigger the bad voodoo-ice magic. Even in the cabin, which had felt like a lifetime ago, wrestling that poor door closed.

Well, that was child's play compared to this.

Blowing snow and ice. So hard and fast she could barely open her eyes. Blinding, that's what it was. A living, breathing fury on this mountain. She watched as pine trees, the ones all covered in heaps of brilliant snow lookin' like an Santa Claus hat without the red, were suddenly bowled over. And, of course, and all that snow came hurtling right at her. Not James, her.

Kate covered her face.

But instead of hitting her, the snow formed around her. Around and around her legs. Her snow pants no longer kept away the cold. Instead, it slipped its way past the smooth fabric and into her body, leaching away her warmth, her fire. Didn't stop there. Oh no, that ice also encased her legs, holding her in place.

All the while the wind kept on pushing. More and more snow, forming around her. One inch, then another.

Faster now.

One foot. Another.

All to hold her there. To keep her in place for...

For Aila's arrival.

Kate felt that certainty right from her numb face to her growing numb toes (though for a different reason, and not one directly related to magic, which was something). Cold was cold, and holy shit was this temperature dropping and dropping *seriously* fast.

"Put these on!"

James tossed her his goggles, and surprisingly, she caught them. Even got them on. Seeing again was a good thing, though it only showed just how screwed they were.

Nowhere to run.

Nothing but forest and snow and trees.

Whatever sun she'd seen earlier, gone. Totally and completely. Nothing but gray clouds, so thick and heavy with anger they were nearly black. No light at all that she could see up there, no hope either.

Hell, not even a cave tucked in just the right spot.

You know, the miracle caves in movies that appeared out of the shadowy snow-fog right when you needed them most. A perfect hiding place to shelter in, to hunker down and let this crazy-ass magic to blow on by. No perfect cave appeared, and her elven senses didn't ping in the direction of one, either.

No Durlan this time to pluck her up and haul her into his nice, ridiculously warm cabin with his meat and garlic stew which had left every inch of her feeling satisfied, full, and alive.

They were well and truly on their own.

And surprisingly, she wasn't afraid.

Instead, Kate felt her senses expand, hone even sharper. An awareness she hadn't realized was even there. A thought, an idea... just out of reach, like a glimpsing the flickering of candlelight in a darkened room.

There was a way out, a way to save them, if only she could just—

"We need to leave!"

James.

James was yelling, pulling her away from that thought, that light, like it'd been snatched up by the wind and tossed about the place like cotton candy. She'd been onto something, and he had to go and just start yelling.

"Why is your mom so mad at me?"

"Are you kidding me? Jesus, Kate! You brought the magi here. Just like she knew you would."

"I didn't—"

Kate snapped her own damn mouth shut.

No, she hadn't been the one who'd turned Aila into the snow queen, but she had kinda given the magi just the opportunity they'd needed.

In fact, Kate remembered full well the last conversation she'd had with Aila, when they'd finally reached the meeting spot of the Gathering. Hiking three days. Every inch of her sore and exhausted and desperately needing to wash her hair with real, actual shampoo. Grandma and James, who'd both been her biggest supporters, who'd believed in her even when she couldn't, had both been so disappointed in her. Disappointed because her magical elf genes hadn't woken up as they'd been expecting. Hoping.

Not Aila, though.

Oh, no. She knew better. She'd known Kate wasn't just hopeless, but a danger. Aila had never liked Kate. Hadn't liked how it was Kate who had this special magic to cross the veil, to reach that misty place between worlds. Hadn't liked that Kate, pretty much, had zero control over said-gift (not like they'd ever given her a chance to practice, either). And of course, she really, *really* hadn't liked the thing Kate had going on with her son.

And, true to character, Aila had zero issue making her feelings known. Each of them. Loudly, and pretty darn mean, too. In fact, at the time she'd been pretty upfront about just how dangerous she thought Kate was—and what the consequences would be.

Like ripping Kate's elven soul right out of her.

Like how Kate pretty much threatened everything the elf-descendants had worked for, bringing back the elves and what-not, heal their fading forest.

And oh, yes—let's not forget how Aila had predicted that Kate would single-handedly restart the war between them and the magi.

The magi who'd been waiting and apparently, frothing at the lips for revenge. Of course, then Kate went and did just that. She'd thrown open the big ol' door for the magi to take over, steal away all the important Gathering members, trap Aila as ice queen…

Right, well.

Perhaps Aila did have a pretty good reason to be mad and all.

Course, if *she* hadn't been a traitor in the first place, ready to hand Kate over to her jerk dad, Severi, then maybe none of this would have happened.

Ha! As if they could sit down and talk things out. You know, get out all those negative feelings, all nasty energy. Start out fresh, maybe end with a little hug.

Yeah. Right.

From the look of things, from the way this winter world was turning into winter scary-land, Aila was all for keeping her last promise to Kate (regardless of what part *she'd* played in this stupid mess): To protect their legacy, she would silence the one person with the power to help them.

Which… meant Kate.

(You'd *think* she'd be doing the smart thing and putting all this stupid energy into hunting down the guy who *actually* did all this and not Kate. But, hey, that's adults for you. As if they could ever take responsibility for their actions.)

Another pile of snow and a whole lot of rock chunks, were flung right at Kate's face. Snow and ice and clumped up bits of dirt, splattered in every direction.

She ducked, or thought she did. It was hard to tell. Hard to feel much at all or even tell that she was moving. Between the ice freezing her from the inside out, the ice doing its darnedest to hold her in place.

Her chest hurt.

Air becoming harder and harder to find, to suck in.

Whether it was from the spell or just that fierce howling wind, she didn't know. Like the wind's whole purpose was to keep her gasping, keep her weak and out of sorts, keep the world spinning. Even… going dark a bit along the edges, which couldn't be a good thing.

James was calling to her again. His hood was thrown back and his blond hair snapped at his head, his neck. He was gesturing and waving for her to follow.

There was a... desperate feeling to the ribbon connecting them. And she had this sense that he wanted to hide, to wait out this storm somewhere. Or maybe dig an igloo or something.

Hide and wait.

Again came that tingling feeling. An awareness, a knowing that she couldn't explain with rational or logical thought or reason.

Just an instinct. A gut knowledge.

Or maybe it was magic.

But she knew, without a doubt, that Aila wouldn't wait. Nor would she let them wait it out, either. Kate knew this truth so clearly. As clearly as she knew her own name. Aila would not let them sit back and let this storm blow on by. Oh, no. Not Aila. She was one determined, really powerful woman (shit, now that she was a winter queen, multiply that by like, a lot).

And as cold as Kate was right then, the more she thought about this awareness, the brighter her flames became. Just a little bit, just warming her center just so. Easing, even in some small way, that strain on her chest, in her lungs.

She felt herself suck in a huge, deep breath of air. Freezing air, for sure, but hey, it was air. And the dizziness, the little black spots that had started to appear (which she hadn't fully noticed), faded.

No, she couldn't just stand there and hope for the best.

Hope that as the swirling snow in front of her began forming into a person, that everything would just magically go away.

Kate knew, without a doubt, that she couldn't stand around and wait for Aila to actually arrive. For her to go from this form of swirling ice and snow, and walk (or glide out) like she was a real person, though a pretty cold one.

Aila who was a total ice person, mind you. Complete with crystals and icicles for hair, and a flowing cape made of nothing but snowflakes locking into place, one after another.

At least, that's the way it looked. Still couldn't quite tell. Still mostly ice.

But Kate remembered really, really darn well what Aila was like as a formerly flesh-and-blood person, and she'd been a force. Seriously. The kinda woman who was both lightning and grace all rolled into one. A woman who ate weakness for breakfast and could launch herself across a whole stream, carting around a fifty-pound backpack, and not even stumble or slip. Not even once. Certainly not get her whole foot doused in the glacier-fed waters like someone else Kate knew.

Oh, and let's not forget Aila never had a wrinkle on her perfectly pressed khakis. Never a single strand of her intricately braided, perfectly golden, locks out of place.

And now, as the ice queen?

No way. This was not at all a fight Kate could win. Not in this lifetime.

Not with her two little dinky flames that were already getting attacked thanks to her impromptu (and failed) kiss with James. Winning against someone who was way, way more scarier than any Elsa—and certainly not the Disney version, either.

Not happening.

Didn't meant she was just gonna curl up and give up, either.

Kate saw Aila's familiar, narrow and pinched mouth slowly take shape, her perpetual displeasure whenever Kate was around. Also the small, malicious upwards curl of her mouth, another expression Kate was quite familiar with.

It was almost as if the woman knew exactly what Kate was thinking.

As if she could feel Kate's heart thumping as she stood there, frozen in all that snow. As if she could sense what the cold from both James and Aila's own winter world was doing to her as it ate its way into Kate, making her weaker, heading right towards her dual flames.

It would be easy to give in, to believe what this woman saw in her.

Because she hadn't been wrong, after all. Kate had gone and done all those things Aila had feared. She was the reason this winter world existed, that the magic of Alfeim Forest was now in the control of the magi, that the entire world around them, continued to move on while they were trapped here.

In ice.

In winter with no light, no hope of escape, as if they'd been the ones who'd fallen into a crevasse. Nothing around by coldness and ice.

Again, so easy to give in, to let go.

Just like it would have been easy to give in during Durlan's black, soul-sucking void that took all those little threads of her apart, strand-by-strand, plucking them away until her flames finally dimmed.

Except, they hadn't.

She hadn't let them flicker out. Hadn't let Durlan win.

And like hell she was going to let Aila, either.

Kate wasn't that same teenage girl Aila knew. The one who'd been left by her mom, who stumbled about with magic and misty veils. Sure, she'd made mistakes, but she'd learned from them. Grown stronger.

And god-damn it, she was going to show this contemptuous, nasty bitch of woman just how much she'd grown.

The wind knocked into Kate so hard and fierce it'd probably make one of those hurricane wind monitors go crazy with envy. It nearly knocked her right off her feet—though it certainly did the trick to loosen all the ice encasing her legs.

Enough that she could move.

That she could act.

Especially since ice Aila hadn't fully formed. Crazy powerful lady that she was, she hadn't thought through all those implications yet. Like throwing down the gloves before she had her magic-mojo up at full. Which meant Kate had time... time to think... to act...

The thought tickled at her.

Time.

All of this, all of it, had been about time. Her going back to that moment in time, to that particular Memory when she'd witnessed Aila making that deal with Severi. Maybe this whole thing, everything that was now happening, wasn't really about Kate.

Maybe... maybe it was about much, much more. More than Kate or anyone else realized.

Aila... who'd been willing to betray her kin, her son, and for what?

Kate hadn't a clue, and it wasn't like she was gonna have a heart-to-heart discussion about it either.

Except, there *was* more to this story.

An important piece. One that could possibly, just maybe, help her stay alive.

All she had to do was think.

Think... while the ice queen and her ice magic were doing their damnedest to freeze her solid, and her own temptation to use about the only magic she knew how to use grew and grew.

It... would be so easy to stop time. Even for a moment.

CHAPTER FIFTEEN

The cold continued to work its way into Kate, like it desperately wanted—no, needed—to. It seeped right through her snow pants as if she were back wearing her ripped cotton jeans again, huddling there and shaking her boots off in nothing but a T-shirt.

Kate fought against the cold. Fought against the panic that swelled within her, making it harder to think. She lost feeling in her toes, fingers, foot, hands. And still the cold continued to spread. Her teeth clattered together like they were about to shake right on out.

So easy, indeed, to take this moment in time and simply hit 'pause.'

Kate felt the veil, that misty world, just beyond her normal, everyday senses. The mist that crept right along the edge of her sight. It was a place that was always there. A shadow world you never saw, or when you did, just caught a glimpse out of the corner of your eye.

And for Kate, her way into the veil was always Alfeim Forest. All she had to do was connect with the forest and she could do this. She could stop Aila and the spell slowly freezing Kate's lungs. The snow holding her stronger and stronger to where she stood.

Alfeim was her way into the veil. That's what Kátheryn had taught her, back in her glade. She'd taught Kate how to connect with the forest until she was breathing alongside it. Feel the gentle rise and fall of the earth as it inhaled, exhaled. The fluttering movement of birds tucked away in trunks and snow burrows, as safe a place they could find, until this harsh winter finally passed.

For Kate... all she had to do, was concentrate... connect with Alfeim, and from there she could see the veil. And through the veil was the choice and the path to see Memories.

All she had to do was concentrate.

Again, the temptation to simply halt Aila where she stood, this half-formed ice sculpture, grab James, and run. Escape. Or smash her with something really hard cause that always worked in movies. Especially the animated ones. Frozen villain falls and smashes into thousands of ice shards.

It would be so easy...

Real easy, in fact...

Kate shook her head.

"No," she whispered.

Her breath, nothing more than a puff of air, a warmth that Aila's storm willingly stole. Kate didn't care.

She'd learned her lesson, thanks. One little glimpse back in time had caused all this, not directly, no, but it would never have happened if she hadn't given Severi just the opening he needed.

There had to be another way, another choice...

She needed to trust in this new awareness. That there was a way and she—honest to God—really did have the answer, even if it was still locked inside her.

And not, *not* using time magic.

Before, she would have been afraid. Afraid to try something different and unusual, afraid to fail. It was a hesitation she'd learned because of her mother, who'd taught her, through omission, to distrust everything and anything that had to do with her heritage.

Not anymore, though. Not now.

Because there *was* something else, something much, much further back in time... something that could actually help her now without actually using that magic... if only she just focused...

Kate's flame flickered.

One thought, then another, came together.

That there had been another time... a time of darkness, when they also had no light. No hope. The elves and their kin. When all would have been lost if not for Kátheryn and her promise—

Brightened.

In particular, *Kátheryn's* flame brightened. The rosy-gold one. She'd suddenly became so bright that, for a moment, it reminded Kate of their missing sun, hidden away by all those dark clouds up high.

There must be some memory of Kátheryn's... one that she didn't have anymore, and yet even still, the simple thought, the reminder of it, felt familiar. Resonated with Kátheryn.

Time... and light...

Kate took a deep breath, as deep as she could, as deep as her slowly freezing lungs would allow.

It wasn't a Memory that came to her (that had certainly been declared as big ol' *forbidden* territory), but... it *was* a sense. The kind of sense you got when you closed your eyes and a smell triggered this whole memory in your mind. Not the full thing. And not an exact memory, either. But a fuzzy one around the edges. A back-and-forth play of light and shadows where you couldn't quite remember what was clear and what wasn't.

And yet the feeling, the sense remained the same. The sense of what happened remained true.

There *had* been a time when there'd been no light. A time long past.

A thousand years in the past, maybe?

So... then why didn't Kátheryn remember? What had happened to *her* memory? And why was it coming now, with Aila Ms. Ice Queen ready to go all winter-wonderland on her?

Kate felt the heat in her chest warm, spreading outwards just a little bit, but enough. Enough to breath a tad bit easier. Enough to push even that small amount of ice and cold away.

Something... felt off. And it was a big something.

A memory of Kátheryn's that had been taken... no... *traded*.

To Durlan. Or no, in this case, Odin.

"Holy shit," Kate whispered to herself.

Promises.

That's what he'd said to Kate. Promises made. He'd been talking about a promise Kátheryn had made to *him*.

Oh man, this was so not just about Aila and Severi and their evil little handshake in the middle of Alfeim Forest. All that darkness surrounding them and the bad-voodoo shadow and what-not. Oh, no. There was a whole hell of a lot more going on...

Which she was totally going to deal with another day. After she'd survived this one.

Cause Aila really, really had no interest in that happening.

And Durlan, or Odin, really, wasn't going to come and save her. He'd made *that* pretty darn clear. But if he hadn't wanted her to know even this much, he wouldn't have said squat about promises owed to him.

A light glinted out of the corner of her eye.

Wait... was that?

Kate blinked, and when she looked closer, squinted her eyes, it was gone. Also, it was hard to see much with the dark goggles on and with all the snow and rock bits flinging about the place.

Still... there was something here and she wasn't about to let Aila's winter storm sidetrack her.

She focused on Kátheryn's rosy-gold flame, as if even this little bit of information, this nugget, was enough. That it could help her now, help her stop Ice Queen Aila without using time magic, cause Aila's snow cape was getting impressively long. Whose fingers were actually starting to look like fingers and not just some twig-like blob.

Think. Think, Kate.

What *could* she do? She, who was nothing? Who kept on screwing up left and right—

Again, the light. A glint of...

Gold.

Like sunlight.

Except, there was no sun.

Kate's hands lifted and touched her chest. She couldn't say why she did this, only that it felt right. And even through her thick, heavy gloves, she felt her heart beat. Felt the warmth in her, and it was growing, was getting stronger.

Without even realizing it, she'd been fighting.

Her flames, warming her, pushing away all the cold, even the magic from James. She'd been fighting.

Time.

Light.

Again came that sense.

She wasn't a lost hope. She could do this.

Her chest continued to warm. Spreading just a little further, reaching to her neck, her belly, pushing back the ice, the frozen magic.

James was still shouting at her. James, who had no idea that all these thoughts and realizations were zipping through her as she was having her internal one-on-one with her flames. He was waving his arms like *she* was the crazy person (which, considering she was still standing in front of the forming, magical ice queen, he wasn't wrong entirely).

He yelled at her to run. To hide.

Just like her mother had always done. Her mother who'd kept running from the truth instead of just accepting all sides of her.

The light and the shadows.

An awareness... just... just out of reach. A thought, an idea, if only she had more time—

Screw it. She was out of time. There was only enough time to jump. Jump with both feet in, right into the deep end, whatever the consequences.

Which was how she usually got into these messed-up situations in the first place.

Good or bad, all she had was this moment, this instinct.

No time for thoughts or doubts. Just enough... to believe.

In the light.

Which she carried... right inside her.

Kate ripped off the goggles James had given her. She needed to see, truly *see*. She searched, her eyes moving fast, feeling every moment tick by. Didn't know what she was looking for, but knew, without a doubt, she'd know it when she saw it.

Ping. Ping.

Ice and snow splattered against her numb face.

She shoved them away as best she could. Squinted. Tried to see.

Needed to focus, to think...

But her head... it sure wasn't coming up with any bright ideas, any brilliant means of escaping some certain icy death magic. Nothing at all here but trees and more trees.

The flames in her chest warmed.

She felt them brighten, felt them push back against the creeping ice.

They urged her to try again. To look again... but not with her mind, but with her heart, her souls. The part that beat with all this living magic.

And just as Kate was about to turn around, ready to give up and just run like hell after James and hoped like hell he had some better plan, she saw it.

Saw her answer.

Another pine tree, older with shriveled, brown branches, was knocked over by that fierce wind. Picked up by its roots and thrown down like a little rag doll. It crashed to the ground, sending up a spray of snow and ice. All the while, Aila and her wind kept on laughing and hackling, as if it already knew the game had been won, that she had won.

Aila, however, was wrong.

Because behind that dying, fallen tree, still standing strong, huddled as it was against all those other taller, older trees, was another. This one which had been waiting there, waiting, just for her...

Kate glimpsed gold.

The golden larch leaves, which had frozen in their fall foliage. Frozen with all the light of the sun absorbing into it. The tree's own last energy before it had closed down for a long winter's sleep, only to awaken when the warmth of spring returned, ready for a new season's growth. Except the spring had returned and the tree had remained frozen all this time.

Frozen in place. Frozen *in time*...

The larch tree with its frozen, golden leaves, was the only color left in this snowy world. But there was still color, still light. It existed. And the sun, as if knowing what would come to pass, what would be needed, had left behind this gift.

A light that had been left there.

For her.

For this moment in time.

CHAPTER SIXTEEN

Of course, to get to the tree and all that light, she still had Aila to deal with.

The ice Aila, who'd opened her eyes.

They were still the same gray as before, the same shade as James's, in fact. But unlike before, Aila's eyes were now encased behind this unmistakable deep blue of thick, thick ice. The kind you'd see staring down into a narrow crevasse on a somewhere glacier, the deep ravine made up of nothing but ice and more ice, packed so tight it took this most brilliant aqua blue. So beautiful, so enticing to just reach out and touch, and that would as soon swallow you whole and that'd be the end of that.

Aila's gaze was just as hard and cold as it had always been, and somehow, even now, still had the power to make Kate feel so tiny, so worthless.

To doubt herself.

"I've been waiting for your return, Katherine Silver." Aila's frosty voice cracked in that frigid air. "And... Kátheryn Silverstar. Ah, yes, so it's true. You've awakened."

A small crack in Aila's ice face.

"Yes, we have been waiting for you. Waiting quite some time for this moment."

The wind picked up. Lugged a couple snowballs at her.

As if that would scare her. She'd faced down Durlan without wetting her pants. Aila was nothing compared to that man. Err... god.

"My name," she said, "is Kate."

"Names no longer have meaning in the cold of winter, as you will soon learn. Just as you will learn the price to pay for your mistakes, for what has happened to our beautiful Alfeim."

Uh-huh, cause all this was *her* fault.

As if Ms. Sneaking Around and making deals with her seriously evil dad was blameless here.

As Aila talked, more of her became solid. Less ice, more person. The strands of her hair become solid, but not the usual blonde as before. Instead, pure, pure white, which made her a heck of a lot scarier looking. Especially with that nasty, mean sneer.

But that didn't mean Kate was going to back down. Not at all.

Kate crossed her arms and glared right back at Aila.

"I get it. You're mad. You never liked me from the start and now really you're mad that I used time magic and my dad went and turned you into the snow queen. Well, guess what? Alfeim showed me the truth. Alfeim showed you meeting with him, you making a deal to hand me over."

Alia straightened. Her white hair fell about her shoulders, landing on this dress of blue silk and snow. Her hair stayed completely still, which was impossible because Kate's hair was thrashing all about the place thanks to that pissed-off wind.

"Alfeim," Aila said, "would never betray me."

"You so sure about that? Especially when it came between you... and Kátheryn?"

Well, that did it.

Talk about a big line drawn in the sand. Err... snow.

The wind picked up.

Thrashed so hard it ripped right into her. Tearing at her clothes, pulling at her jacket as if it was determined to yank the thing right off her and leave her standing naked in the snow with nothing but her boots on—

"Mother!"

It was James. He was shouting and shoving his way closer to Kate. He pushed past ice and snow that suddenly seemed to reach his hips, and even as she watched, more piled on, as if purposefully slowing him down. To keep him from reaching Kate.

"Mother! This is not her fault and you know it. It's yours. It's *all* of ours. You can't—"

"You have no longer have a say in this conversation, my son. Your fate is sealed."

Aila flicked her hand, and James went flying.

It was like his whole body got snatched up by that thrashing wind. He was there, then he was gone. He flew several feet in the air before crashing. It was like an entire field separated them. All she could see was the snarling snow and ice.

No movement. No James.

"James!"

He didn't answer her.

Aila did, though.

"My plan was perfection, you foolish, foolish girl. Everything was ready, everything was in place... until you."

Aila moved forward, the snow hardening into ice as she walked, though her feet, Kate noticed, her dress, weren't yet fully formed. Just a swirling mass of wind and snow and ice. Even now, she saw Kate as insignificant. A silly child with silly little powers.

She hadn't noticed the light.

Hadn't noticed the larch tree.

"You showed up," Aila said. "You changed my son, made him feel as Aevar did. You, who had the gift to walk the veil, did so without care or concern for the rest of us."

"You mean, for *your* plan," Kate said. "Yours and my dad's."

"He would have been handled," Aila said, dismissively. "Just as he has always been, time and time before."

Jesus. Just how many times had this little game been played out? And for that matter, how the hell did Aila know so much about it?

Kátheryn seemed pretty darn clueless on that matter (though, she had gone and traded away her memories, so there was that).

Still, as pissed as Aila was right now, certainly the way the wind was tearing into her, the way the ice magic was boring into Kate, trying its damnedest to reach her flames, Aila was nowhere near as scary as Durlan, and Kate had stood up to him.

Odin. The All Father.

She took comfort in that, especially as it was now just her and the ice queen.

Aila moved closer.

Now just a few feet away from Kate.

"After all this time, all my long years of waiting, everything had been in place. Everything. And if you hadn't opened a gateway, hadn't stepped through time itself and unleashed all that wild magic, *I* would now be walking alongside my kin. I would have retaken my place among them."

With each sharp word, the storm thrust snow at Kate. Ice pelted her face. So cold it would have made her wince and shiver except she wasn't feeling much at all, right now.

Which was way scarier than Aila was.

She had to fight this magic.

"Rightfully mine," Aila whispered, "ever since we entered this world. I will have it back, at any means, however long I must wait."

Kate shoved hair and ice out of her way. She really hadn't a clue what Aila was talking about, but then that could be some of the elf history she was missing, and she was surely missing quite a bit.

She looked across that distance, searching for any sign, anything at all, of James.

No movement. Nothing but the wind and the snow.

Could she reach him? Did she dare? Risk drawing Aila's attention back to him?

No... no, she couldn't. Just like she couldn't risk Aila seeing the larch tree and all that golden light it held in safe keeping for Kátheryn, for this moment.

Golden light, which was Kátheryn's birthright while the coldness, the shadows, had been Aila's.

"Instead of royalty," Aila said, "I am trapped in this form. And my *son* is trapped in ice of your own creation. While the others... taken."

Aila closed her eyes and perhaps, just maybe, shuddered.

As if she felt even a tiny bit of remorse for what had happened, maybe, just maybe seeing that her hands weren't exactly clean here. Cause seriously, did she really not think this hadn't been her dad's plan from the beginning?

"You know," Kate said, "we could still do something about all that, you know. Work together."

She had to keep Aila talking. Had to keep her focus on Kate... not on James... not on the true threat.

The threat of Kate and her dual flames, the warmth as it spread through her, faster and faster, pushing against all that ice, all that magic.

Aila hadn't noticed; so focused on her anger, on the dreams that could never ever be—because Kate wouldn't let them come true.

Not now. Not ever.

Aila's gray-ice eyes narrowed. "Always a joke with you."

Or, she could just piss the woman off more. That certainly was one of Kate's superpowers.

"You, who never believed," Aila snapped. "I should never have allowed you to even enter Alfeim, regardless of what Severi promised. I should have waited for another to be reborn with Kátheryn, another who I could have controlled and shaped, right from the beginning."

"Like your son?"

Kate had no idea where that question from, or why. Just... just that it was there and it needed to be said, spoken.

A question that fell at Aila's feet. Her gray eyes, still so much like James' even though they were encased behind all that ice—

"It is better, this way. Certainly if he'd never met you. Never awakened that awful part of himself. But it has and that cannot be undone. What I will do is rectify my mistake. At last. For this long year, I've waited Kate Silver. Kátheryn Silverstar. To end you both."

Which was Kate's cue to boogie.

Kate didn't call out to James, didn't warn him about her crazy plan.

For once, time was pretty much the essence here. Also, there was no real plan.

Just an instinct.

A magic that called to her, that hummed through her. Before she even realized what her body was doing, she was moving. She broke through the ice encasing her legs. A thousand shards shot out in all directions. Some maybe hit her, cutting and slicing through her pants, but she couldn't tell. Didn't care, either.

Kate was running.

Running across that snow, running right towards the fallen pine tree with its brown and shriveled branches, its trunk snapped in half. Broken, that ancient tree, all so it could help her.

With every step she took, she felt a growing awareness. Almost like a shift in the earth, in that dirt buried underneath all that cold, all that ice and snow. A touch of life, of green, though not growing. Sleeping, but now finally, after all these long months, stirring, stretching, waking.

Alfeim Forest was finally waking up.

CHAPTER SEVENTEEN

The trees, their roots buried so far down in that earth, hidden under snow and ice and rock, shifted and moved. They felt Kate, her feet running on top that frozen surface, and in turn she felt them. A tingling that shot up her feet, right through the heavy fabric of her snow boots, her snow pants. What magic those trees had left, hunkered down in their roots, hidden away from both the magi and Aila—urged her to run. To keep going.

And she did.

Hoped, too, that they heard her, heard her as she answered with her heart and both her souls—she wouldn't let them down.

Just beyond the fallen pine tree, his noble sacrifice, who'd shielded the larch tree, keeping it safe and tucked away from Aila's rage and cold, cold winter, was the golden glow.

A light Kate could use.

Not that she knew how exactly, only that she could.

Kate's boots pounded as hard and fast as she could on that iced-over snow. Snow that shifted into sleek, black ice even as her foot lifted off.

Aila's magic. Her doing.

Aila was not about to fail, not now in the middle of all her winter, not after Kate went and screwed up her apparently super-intricate, really long, thought-out plan.

Aila knew Kate would slip on the ice, would fall, and that would be the end of that. After all, she *was* the one who went leaping over a stream and actually landed with both feet in it.

Hell, Kate knew she was gonna fall, and if she were in James's head right now, he'd know it, too.

Kate was the most sorriest excuse for an elf-descendant. Hands down. No question about it. She was the biggest klutz that was ever born to beings who were pretty much the definition of grace.

And yet, here she was, running across an entire field of slick, magical ice, thinking she was gonna outwit the snow queen herself. Oh, and *not* fall?

Laughable, at best.

At worst, she'd be hauled up to a hospital with more than a few broken bones. If they weren't trapped in this cursed winter scary-land, anyway.

All these thoughts went zipping by in just a single fraction of moment. Then, that moment was gone, and Kate's foot was slamming down towards that gleaming, glistening ice—

She felt the moment her thick gripping treads met slick, perfectly smooth ice. The kind of ice that had the perfect amount of give, of wetness, to make you slip, to lose all forward momentum.

Kate felt herself sliding, falling. Her arms pinwheeling forward—

No.

She was *not* going to fall. She was not going to land on her ass and disappoint everyone. Not scary Durlan. Not James. She would not be that girl anymore. The girl who kept falling. The girl who sloshed through streams instead of leaping over them. *That* was the old her. The her who didn't believe, who grumbled and gave up.

Kate had promised to fix this, and she would.

She concentrated all her focus, everything she had, on that golden larch tree with its full branches like a crown gleaming off the sun's light even though there was no sun.

Focused on that light...

One foot coming down, then another.

And instead of her body resisting the sudden motion, the sudden out-of-control force between foot and ice, she went with it. She went with the flow of energy, of movement.

Didn't fight against it, didn't fight the ice and physics or whatever the heck it was. She just... gave in to instincts.

And instead of falling, she glided.

Her momentum sprang her forward, following the direction the ice itself. Where it dictated, she went. Slightly to the left, and she went with it. Then again to the right. Always moving forward, always using her own force to springboard her forward, but never against the ice.

She allowed both to carry her forward. Relied purely on movement and instinct. Something that was so beyond her rational mind that just the thought of figuring out how the heck she was not falling flat somewhere on her ass turned her mind to mush.

The why and the how didn't matter.

All that mattered was reaching the golden glow of the larch tree.

A tree that Aila had seen.

Her raging shriek followed right at Kate's heels. The same heels that flew over the ice. Feet, arms, legs, everything, her whole entire self, working together. Every bit of her focusing down until they were one movement, one goal.

Aila's scream careened off all those snowed-in trees, the high rock walls off in the distance with their sharp, pointed crags.

But Kate didn't stop.

Didn't look back either, not even when she heard James shout... in pain. As if Aila had turned her frustration onto him, using everything she could to get Kate to turn around, to hesitate.

I'm sorry, James.

She couldn't stop. Not if they both wanted to live.

Not that Kate knew what her plan was or what her flames had in mind with the larch's light. In fact, she hadn't a clue. But whatever really cool plan her flames had going on, it was gonna be *amazing*.

Why?

Because she had two souls in her who were kinda feeling a bit pissed with everything that had happened, everything that had happened when she'd accidentally created that gateway. And even more important, she wasn't fighting who she was. Not anymore.

Again, her foot touched onto the ice, then glided right off it.

Aila sent an entire branch hurling right at Kate's head (a branch that was nearly the size of half a tree, seriously). She ducked. It brushed past her wind-snapping hair and grazed the little tip of her left ear.

And still she kept going forward.

The snow, once again, bit into her face. So very, very cold. Cold enough to make her pause and wonder... were her flames enough? Here she was, making this mad-dash across the snow plains to reach some tree. And when she got there? Then what??

It wasn't like Kátheryn or her rosy-gold flame were using their awesome powers of like, communication, to—you know—communicate what the heck she was supposed to do next.

All she did was jump... with both feet in again.

Her running slowed, if only a tad.

It was enough, though. Enough for Aila to sense this. To find her way in.

"You don't belong here."

Aila's shrill voice echoed all around her, in every snowflake and icicle. Even in the cold air she now breathed. It was like again, she could read Kate's mind. As if she had some sixth sense about saying the right things to trip her up, to make her doubt herself.

"You never belonged here," Aila pushed on. "Even James knew. That was why, in the end, he couldn't be near you. Couldn't touch you."

Maybe... she hadn't belonged.

Again, her steps slowed. Allowed more snow and ice to splat against her snow pants.

The snow and the ice underneath her, it shifted. Continued to become so slick it was practically gleaming, desperate for her to take that one step, that one, unfocused step, and to fall. Fall as everyone had expected of her. Always.

The trees, all their branches, snow-laden as they were, bent towards her. Shivered and shook.

The trees, the whole forest around her, waking up and... flinging snow... not at Kate, but... behind her. At... at Aila.

Kate shoved hair out of her face and kept running. Because Aila wasn't wrong. Back then, back when she was trying to understand who she was, when she was thrust into a world of elves and magic, both which had apparently already had it out for her, she hadn't belonged. In fact, a huge part of her had resisted just that.

Because she was afraid. Afraid to take that leap, afraid to open her heart only to discover that no, even here, even now, she was different.

Weird.

Other.

But now, that didn't matter. She was both, weird and other, different than even her kin. Even compared to James. And it didn't matter.

She belonged.

Belonged to her grandmother, belonged to Kátheryn and this strange heritage. Belonged to the trees of Alfeim.

Kate's foot connected with ice, and instead of slipping, she sprang forward.

So close now, so close to the golden larch trees and its frozen leaves. Nearly... there...

"No!" Aila screamed at her.

The force of Aila's anger grew.

She hurled both wind and ice at Kate. They sliced right at her face. Some missed. Many hit their mark. Tiny cuts, burning and freezing all at the same time, a living magic that matched the coldness in Aila's heart.

Blood slipped down her cheeks and she felt the drops starting to freeze, felt the magic desperately working to dull her flames, to win.

Kate's steps slowed, even as she fought against it. But it was like Aila had thrown every shard of winter, every piece of her strength, her magic, right into Kate.

Desperate to stop her. Desperate to not lose everything *she'd* dreamed of for all these very long, very lonely years...

Kate couldn't let Aila win. Wouldn't let her win.

"No," she whispered to herself.

Again, she touched down on the ice, sprang forward. Closer and closer to the frozen light of the larch tree.

Nearly there.

But still, too slow.

"Do you really think he loves you?" Aila asked.

Taunted.

"Do you think it's you that holds his heart? Do you think it's *you* who he *believes* in? Or is it her? An elf, who both know you could never compete against?"

A foot slipped, just a little.

And like a shark sensing blood, Aila attacked. Full force. Nothing held back.

"Don't you remember what he said, when he finally crashed into that dinky cabin? The look he gave you. The contempt. He stopped believing in you, he stopped loving you. How else could the ice have taken over his heart?"

It was enough. More than enough.

Enough to create this one tiny sliver of doubt. It had little to do with love. Kate wasn't an idiot. She knew damn well they hadn't worked *that* part out yet, but... they hadn't been given the time. Or the chance.

But... she'd always thought... that James believed in her.

And yet, from the moment she returned, he'd shown time and time again, that he didn't anymore. And maybe that he'd never believed in her at all.

Kate felt her balance shift. Felt her body slide to the left while her feet went to the right. Her arms, pinwheeling, pushing for balance, anything and everything to stay in control.

But there was no control, and she felt herself lose that one piece, the most important piece of all:

Her confidence.

CHAPTER EIGHTEEN

Kate was slipping. Falling.

And the wind, of course, was doing its darnedest to help her along. Pushing and shoving at her from all directions. It tore at her hair, her jacket. Ice and bits of rocks bit into her face, pinged against her pants. Heck, even ripped through that expensive, synthetic fabric in a few places because they were so sharp and so god-damn determined.

All the while, Aila laughed.

Merciless. Joyful. All those years of planning and plotting, of betraying her own kind—finally, it was here. As Kate slipped all over the ice, her confidence flying straight out the window, this moment right here, was everything Aila had been waiting for. Her celebratory moment. All she needed now was a show of ice-themed fireworks, maybe even cue the Disney music and let it all go—

And you know what?

In another time, in another place, Kate *would* have given in.

Would have accepted, hands down, that Aila was right, and that Kate had no place here, here in this world of elves and magic and... James.

But that—

Was bullshit.

The before-her, the her who her mom had dumped off in Montana, honked her horn and let her shotgun-wielding grandma actually handle the rough bits, *that* Kate would have curled up and asked for a ride home. But *this* Kate, the new Kate with her own little living flame, its silver tinge right along with the blue and green, like it was the living forest itself, *this* Kate was a whole different story.

She belonged, god damn it, and she was seriously, seriously done being blamed for everything. And thinking that everything was her fault. Because you know what? This, this right here, Aila going all apeshit winter-crazy?

This was not her fault.

Kate did not slip on the ice as Aila desperately wanted. Needed.

Instead her boot touched down and she sprang off that slick surface, the ice that would probably freeze her tongue if she did something stupid and touched it.

She wasn't slowing down anymore. Oh, no. Instead, she was gaining speed cause now, now she was just pissed off.

"You know what?" Kate yelled back. "To hell with you. You don't like what my dad did to you? Fine. What the *hell* are you going to do about it?"

This time a tree fast-pitched itself right at Kate.

Yep. A full-on tree.

And by fast pitch, she meant like a softball careening towards her at seventy-five miles per hour.

And Kate, new Kate here, she who was in touch with her inner-elfness, totally pulled one of those *Lord of the Rings*, Legolas moments, and hopped and skipped and then *slid down* the full-on length of the trunk. Her hair wasn't this perfect wave behind her or anything, it was sticking to her forehead and nose, but this also wasn't the movies. Though she did manage to *not* pump up her arms and say something incredibly childish and silly like *woot-woot*... if just... barely.

But Kate wasn't done.

Oh, no. It was *her* turn to screw with Aila.

"If you don't like what the hell Severi did, turning you into an ice queen and all, maybe you should take it up with *him*."

The magic within Kate, her flames, suddenly glowed.

Brightened.

Their warmth pushed against all that ice still inside her. Yes, the ice and the magic that still lingered there, left over from her failed attempt at kissing James and saving him. Also from Aila's raging storm and the snow that didn't care anything about those super special synthetic fabrics and leached right into her body, stealing away every ounce of heat it could. Even now still trying to steal her confidence, her heart.

But it wasn't just Kate's flames that had brightened through this moment.

This moment of her simply running across a field of snow... as if anything involving magic and ice and a pissed-off mother-in-law (ha, as if she and James were actually an item, let alone married) were a simple thing. But their ribbon, the gold one connecting her and James, the connection they'd always shared, the one she'd felt the moment she first laid eyes on him while hiding behind that box of Captain Crunch cereal with that ridiculous captain in his too-big blue hat... their ribbon, it glowed, too.

And shone brighter and stronger than ever before.

In fact, their gold looked just like the larch tree, just like the sun she could almost imagine so high up in the sky, way past those dark, heavy clouds. All she had to do was close her eyes and she could see them both.

The sun.

Their ribbon. Both glowing with light and... and magic.

And she heard James. Heard his voice, filled with pain as if it took everything he had to whisper this one, single word:

Go.

She felt him, then. Felt his breath tickling against her cheek as if he stood right beside her.

Go.

So, she did.

She ran.

Her feet connected against the ice. No longer out of control. No longer slowly but moving faster and faster still. Faster even than before.

James believed in her.

She felt it. Something she'd thought long gone, something she thought could never be repaired or reclaimed. Broken and destroyed when she opened that gateway in time, when she'd seen Alfeim's Memory, and left him behind. But... it was still there. His belief in her, and even though it had been buried deep under all that ice, was still there.

Kate could do this. She was *meant* to do this.

The warmth in her chest grew.

Faster.

One foot pushing off the ice. Her body, one fluid, even graceful movement, as she dodged past another tree.

As she moved, the light of her flames, their warmth, spread. Expanded. Moved into her chest, inhaling and exhaling. Pushing out the ice that didn't belong. Then to her face, her nose. Finally, her lips... they were no longer frozen and numb.

And the warmth kept on spreading until it was not just within her but reaching out. Reaching out into the forest itself, right into Aila's winter world.

All the while, Aila threw every bit of her magic she could at Kate. The snow and ice pelted her, and the moment it did, it melted.

Little sizzles of steam drifting off her skin, her clothes.

That's all it was.

Steam.

Light sparkled in the air around Kate, and she saw the answering glow from the larch tree. Its leaves brightening.

Answering the summons.

Answering... her.

Her magic.

Her flames kept on brightening and in her heart, she heard Kátheryn's voice...

"Use the tree. Use its light."

Whatever the heck that meant.

Kate might be more in tune with her elfness, but Kátheryn

certainly still hadn't learned the fine art of speaking clearly and skipping over all the cryptic bits. But... whatever. She'd just wing it.

Like always.

She ran harder, faster. Arms pumping up then back. Nearly there...

"*Use it.*"

Kate ripped the gloves off her hands. And while a training manual would have been nice, she'd figure it out, just like she always did. Because she knew she wasn't alone.

Alfeim Forest.

James.

Even her grandmother, wherever she was.

Each of them were with her. Each of them believed in her. And most important of all, she believed in herself.

Kate's fingers brushed the ice encasing the tree, the same ice that had frozen solid over all those golden leaves. And then she felt her own heat, her flames grow until they were a living warmth inside her chest. The ice melted under her touch. Melted in a brilliant steam of light and warmth.

And she felt the rough, coarse bark. The life sleeping there, all the water and nutrients, the hundreds of paths reaching up through the tree's tallest branches and then down again to its deepest root.

The tree stirred. Stretching, almost, from a deep, deep sleep.

A branch shifted on its own and brushed her cold, battered, and bruised cheek.

"I'm here," she whispered.

Then her palm pressed fully against the tree, and her magic, that glowing heat within her, spread outwards. Raced up the tree in brilliant golden spirals. All the way to the very top of the tree, diving into those thick branches and the rustling gold of fall-colored leaves. And as soon as her spirals hit the top, they raced right back down again. Diving into the earth in a flurry of gold... but not just gold, no. There were rose-colored ones, another a brilliant, aqua blue, and yet another, another that was green and simply felt like the forest.

They were the colors of her flames, of hers and Kátheryn's. This, this was *their* magic. Together.

And this larch tree, with all its life there, suddenly woke up.

And for just that moment, that split second between the tree waking up and her exhaling a breath she hadn't realized she'd been holding, Kate felt the misty world. The coldness as it licked her cheeks. The spindly fingers of fog as it brushed her hair. A place of fog and shadows. It was there, and then it wasn't.

As Kate let out her breath, the magic of the tree, all its golden sunlight that had sat there, trapped and sleeping, waiting for this moment, exploded outwards. And Kate found herself standing in the middle of summer.

CHAPTER NINETEEN

S ummer.

Honest to God summer.

"You have *got* to be kidding me," Kate said. "Please don't tell me I did it again."

All that snow, gone. The pine trees standing tall, their branches curving under the grace of their own pine needles and not because they were carting around a couple hundred extra pounds. No white Santa hats. No slick ice covering the ground.

In fact, there were wildflowers everywhere.

Purples and blues, yellows, too. It looked like a sea of color where she stood, a rainbow that used to be in the sky and decided it'd look better on the ground, right amidst all the green, springy grass. Not that she'd seen anything like this last summer when she'd carted herself and her backpack off into the middle of Alfeim Forest in the hot summer of July, back when it had been stealing just about every speck of water it could, the ground and the air itself so damn thirsty.

That summer had looked nothing at all like this.

Like... well, like magic.

The flames within her danced quietly, as if they wanted to answer her... or maybe they did and she just didn't speak their language. Which was most likely the case.

She thought about poking Kátheryn. You know, nudge her for an actual answer. But nope, the elf soul in her was silent. Not a worried silent, you know, knees quivering like when Durlan had plucked her out of the snow and then grilled her later in his warm cabin, with all his lovely, lovely stew. Just the thought of that all that garlic and meat made her stomach grumble (who knew a god could cook, right?).

But Kátheryn was totally and completely silent. No helpful hint, either. Just this content little feeling in her belly. That was all.

Which, pretty much stayed true to form with how elves seemed to operate, at least from Kate's experience.

Cryptic jerks, the lot of them. And they wondered why she kept on messin' up and making mistakes.

Kate kicked a rock with her snow boots, which were growing quite warm around her toes. She slowly let go of the tree, not quite ready to ditch her boots, and the rough bark scraped her hand.

Bits of bark fell away. Flaked off like... like it was dying.

Wait... what?

She glanced up.

Her larch tree with its beautiful light, the light that had been frozen by Aila's spell, trapped there and just waiting for Kate to come home, to end this winter... it was gone. It wasn't gold any longer but instead brown and dying.

Leaves shriveled as she watched, crumpling in on each other and falling down. Falling like a sad, brown snow.

They fell on her hair, on her snow jacket. One rested on her nose for a moment, as if saying farewell, then fell off when a light breeze kissed it away.

She didn't realize until that moment that she was crying.

Kate reached up, pushed away one tear, then another. Her heart aching.

The forest had trusted in her, had known she would return to save it, to end the winter, and this, this was the price. The tree's life. It seemed like there was always a price when it came to elves and their magic, and she really, really didn't like it.

Especially since she did this. This, right here.

She reached out again and touched the larch tree. More bark fell away. More and more until the wind finally blew again. And, like blowing out a candle flame, the tree, her tree, was gone. Carried off by the wind with all its spirals and updrafts, taking away the flakey bark and crumpled branches. Simply, gone. All that remained were the shriveled leaves along the forest floor, laying there right amidst all those wildflowers.

It felt like both a reminder and a promise.

"I... I did this."

"Yes," Aila answered. "You did."

Kate spun around. Hair whipped her face.

She'd thought she was alone. Just her and her tree. She hadn't heard Aila approach, which just went to show you she wasn't all cool elf-ness yet (or ever).

But this... this was no longer Aila, the snow queen.

Aila's hair was still brilliant white, not the darker blond it used to be, the color that had looked so like James. Gone, however, were her snow robe and dress. They were replaced instead by her tan khakis, the same ones she'd worn that summer a year before, when Kate went and screwed with time. And just like then, her pants still hadn't a wrinkle on them. Not a single misplaced crease, nor a single speck of dirt on her face, either. And her hands? They looked like she'd cleaned them good in the glacier-cold waters that Kate could hear nearby... that soft, soothing fall of water trickling down and out through some underground crease in the mountains.

Aila, like always, looked perfect.

Kate, on the other hand, looked the sight.

Hair sticking out in every which way. Super tangled as well. The kind that required the sharp snipping of scissors if she ever had any hope of reclaiming her hair from its knotted colony. Then there was her face, with all the cuts and bruises (thanks to Aila here), which probably looked way worse (and scarier) than her hair.

Which was saying something.

Also, Kate was about as complete a contrast to Aila's beautiful face as you could get. The woman must have some spell tucked away, something to give this light dusting of make-up (not that Kate had ever seen a sign of lip gloss, mind you). But seriously, the woman sure looked it. Cheeks all rosy and perfect. Not a single blemish or even the *sign* of an emerging pimple.

Also, her face resembled the living again. You know, losin' that too-pale look of snow.

And perhaps most important of all, her eyes... they were gray again. Only gray. Not a speck of that icy-blue in sight. They were still pretty serious looking, though. Still pretty... annoyed and frustrated as she stared at Kate (not quite glared, but right there on that cusp). But this time... Aila's stare didn't have quite the same intensity has before. Or that cold animosity that had been trying really, really hard to kill her.

You know, like a minute ago.

Not that Kate trusted this woman for a second. She backed up a step, reached out for her tree and all its glowing light magic before realizing that it was gone and she was again, alone.

Great.

"I thought I stopped you," Kate said.

"You did. You ended my winter."

Aila moved forward, her hiking boots not making a single sound even as she stepped on the crumpled, crunchy leaves of Kate's larch tree. The leaves that were the last sign that it had ever stood there. She had this silly sense to yell at Aila to get her grubby feet off.

"You ended my winter," Aila said, "and in doing so, you did it again. You paused Time."

"I did *not*."

Truly. Seriously. She'd been so careful. She'd only used *her* flames, well, and the tree.

Kate shook her head and backed up another step. Mostly cause Aila was still walking towards her and the urge to keep on living was quite powerful (she remembered quite well the size of that *last* tree Aila had flung at Kate). But also, too, because the thought of screwing with time again.

Oh no—

"I didn't," Kate said. "It was all me. My magic. Using the tree, its light. I didn't use a Memory. I didn't go back in time—"

"No. But as I said, you paused it."

There was no lie in Aila's voice and her words, even if Kate really, really hated to admit it... they felt right. True.

"Son of a bitch," Kate swore. "Is *anyone* going to tell me how this shit works?"

Was she frustrated? Oh. Beyond belief.

She'd followed her instincts. Tried so hard to do the right thing, but every single god-damn time it was the *wrong* thing. And Severi—oh, no. If she'd screwed with time magic... what could he do this time? To Grandma? To, to James—

Kate snapped her head in the direction she'd seen him last, desperate to see him. Find him. But... no James. Just wildflowers and pine trees and the sun glinting through their dark green needles. The golden rays winking as they began their slow descent to the west and those even farther off, craggy mountains.

But, no James.

"James," she whispered.

"He's not here."

Kate glared at her. "I can see that."

"Can you? Truly?"

Aila's gray eyes flicked to Kate's chest... right to where her flames were, and where their golden ribbon, hers and James, connected.

Kate sucked in a breath—couldn't believe that she was taking advice from the woman who'd just tried to kill her with a freakin' tree —and breathed in that clear, warm mountain air. So pure and crisp, with just a hint, like a small, stray spark, of a coming thunderstorm.

Durlan, maybe? Pissed and heading on over, riding a raging thundercloud cause she went and screwed up again? Or maybe he was finally gonna take out Aila? No. That didn't feel right. He'd told her this was *her* problem to fix, not his. She believed that. And the spark didn't feel angry either, just... just what was.

A natural way of life here in the high mountains. Not quite magical, not really. Although you could argue everything here, especially in Alfeim Forest, had a touch of magical to it.

Certainly felt like it.

And that's all Kate really had to go by. Her instincts. What felt right, what felt wrong, and when... when she had no better options, to just go with what felt the closet to right even if it was still ultimately wrong.

Like... using time magic.

She squeezed her eyes, stifling a groan.

Oh man, was Durlan going to yell at her. Again.

But what really mattered was that James, at least at this moment, the ribbon, hers and James's... *was* still there. She couldn't sense him anywhere close by, but it was there. She didn't feel any pain from him, and most important of all, it no longer felt cold.

Kate reached up, touched her chest. Smiled.

Consequences. Choices.

She'd stopped Aila's winter and in doing so, she'd stopped the curse eating away James's light.

He was okay. She knew this, without a doubt. *Felt* it. There was no more ice magic cursing him. No more cold taking advantage of the hurt she'd done to him. Well, the hurt was probably still there, but that was okay. That was something they, maybe, could work through.

If given half a chance, anyway.

If Aila, Ms. Still Staring Over There, didn't try and kill her.

Again.

CHAPTER TWENTY

Kate lowered her hand. She took one last deep breath of that fresh, pure mountain air, heard the glacier-fed waters trickling through the mountain, the song of birds flittering about the trees, gave herself this one small moment of peace, of knowing that, in this moment, everything was alright... that it would be alright. That James was safe.

And then, she faced Aila.

"Are you going to try and kill me? Or are you going to tell me how badly I screwed up this *time*."

And yes, the word *time* was deliberate.

Aila shrugged her long, pure white hair over her shoulders. So silky and smooth, she looked like she belonged on some shampoo commercial, It really wasn't fair.

"Neither," Aila said. "You did exactly as you needed to. Exactly as I needed you to."

Kate blinked. Then she blinked again.

Clearly, she hadn't heard right.

"Wait, wait. Hold up a sec. *You* needed me? You tried to kill me!"

Aila, the really, really not nice lady that she was, smiled. No seriously, she *smiled*. And not the twisted, cruel one, the one she pretty much reserved for Kate and *only Kate*. This was an honest-to-God smile.

If she could trust it. Which she didn't.

"Of course, I wanted to kill you," Aila said. "You threatened everything. You ruined everything."

"Oh. Well, then."

She made it sound all so matter-of-fact, like everything that happened was just some annoying hair out of place on her shoulders and she was just gonna shrug the darn thing right into place. Nor was she denying it, either, which Kate hadn't expected.

"Everything you had done," Aila said, "all my feelings for you, your presence in Alfeim, the way you twisted James and led the way for his Aevar to return. That was all Severi's spell needed to trap me. He trapped me in a cold rage of my own creation and there wasn't a thing I could do about it. Or to change it."

Her gray eyes *did* flash this time. Like a mix of storms and lightning.

"A price he will dearly pay for now that I'm free."

Kate could taste the magic in the air. This super-charged sense that made her tangled hair stand up on end. Like although Aila might be out of the whole winter-spell thing she hadn't quite gotten her control back. Certainly not of her emotions.

Then the moment was gone, and Aila was making her way closer, though this time, she seemed to step more carefully around the larch tree's shriveled leaves.

"I might have been trapped in my cold winter, but I knew enough to remember that time magic caused this mess. Only time magic could fix it."

"But I didn't use—"

"Didn't you? Didn't you see the veil before you woke the sleeping larch? Before you used its own light with your own? The mist? The shadows?"

Kate's mouth went dry.

"Its cold touch, so much colder than my own winter?"

"Umm... kind of."

Aila nodded. "The veil. You walked it, if only briefly. You touched it enough to pause time because how *else* could you have used the light in the tree? A light that had been frozen in time?"

"You're here now. I didn't ask you to come here."

Nor had Kate touched her, at least directly, like she had with the larch tree. Of course, she had been standing in all that snow at the time.

"I was meant to be here."

Aila's face twisted again, no mistake the anger there. She was clearly still not cool with everything that had happened, certainly with Kate, regardless of how she was trying to pass it off like no biggie.

Cause, it was.

She, the powerful elf-descendant who, no question about it, had one hell of an old, powerful elven soul living in her (royalty from the way she'd been talking back as Snow Queen back there). And she was also pretty pissed at Kate because she *had* ruined all her carefully laid out plans. Plans Kate had seen, or at least hinted about in the forest's Memory. The damn thing that got her into this mess... and that... unknowingly... changed the course of everything.

Aila's plans. Those had failed. And when they did, it instead gave Severi the opportunity to do his own little bit of nastiness.

"There's no fixing this," Kate said, the realization hitting her. "I can't go back. I can't go back to Kátheryn's glade and... change everything."

Change it back so none of this would have ever happened. So the Gathering members would still be, you know, gathering together with all their coolers and clicking open their beer bottles. Grandma and James, both safe, both waiting back at camp for her.

Who knew where they even were.

Grandma.

Kate still had to find her, or what had even happened to her. Durlan hadn't said and neither had James. But it wasn't just about Grandma. She still had to find all the Gathering members and return things... well, not as they'd been before, that was clearly off the table, but she needed to fix this.

All of it.

Even if those Gathering members still might not like her, still might not like that she had this magic and that she, at least kinda, could control it. A little, anyway. She might still have to fight for Kátheryn and her soul to remain as they were, but she would.

Because she was done running.

"No," Aila said, "no, you can't go back. You can't simply 'fix' this like it never happened. Time must never be changed, Kate Silver. And if you tried, I'd kill you, right here, right now."

Kate huffed. "Get in line. I'd imagine Durlan would be here in an instant throwing a lightning bolt at my ass."

"Durlan?" Aila's eyes widened. The gray just turning just a tad paler. "Yes... of course... of course he would be here."

Wait... Aila hadn't known about Durlan? She'd been the one busting down his cabin door and she hadn't known about him? About him being Odin?

Oh... maybe that was supposed to be a secret and Kate had gone and let that one out of the bag...

She swore to herself. Why, oh why, did people keep expecting her to not be *her*?

Aila shook her head. "It does not matter. He has had business here for many years. It was only a matter of time before he showed up. The point is, of where we are right now. This pause in time. It was created by your magic and it's giving me... this chance. Enough of one, anyway, to explain."

"You tried to kill me," Kate said. "With a tree. Two of them."

"I did. I was... angry."

Oh, as if that just went and explained *everything*.

"I waited for you," Aila said. "It was all I could do. Just wait... wait until time caught back up. For you to step back into the timeline, if you ever would. Do you think James's curse started as you saw it? No. No, it grew ever so slowly as he waited for you to return, and you... you didn't."

Now that got her heart twisting. Especially because she had considered staying. Just hiding out because it was the safe thing to do.

Aila stopped a few feet from Kate, standing there amidst the blue and purple wildflowers, their spiraling petals, and of course, the brown leaves of the larch.

One lifted off the ground in the gentle wind, lightly touched Kate's shoulders as if it wanted to stay, even for a bit longer, before slowly drifting away.

Far away.

"And then you finally arrived," Aila said. "You took your sweet time as always, as if no one or nothing else mattered to whatever silly crusade you saw yourself on. So, yes, I tried to kill you. With the winter spell on me, it was all I could do."

"Yes, about that, and don't think you can lie, cause I saw you and my dad in the Memory—"

"Of course, you did. That is how we ended up in this place, in this time. You saw only what I wanted Severi to see, just as you only saw what *he* wanted me to see. As if enemies, or allies, would ever be truly honest with each other. Including your Kátheryn."

"What?"

"She knew this truth about you. By the great goddess Hel below, we *all* knew. The only way to get you to do anything, certainly anything in a miniscule, productive direction, is to force your hand."

That wasn't a nice thing to say, which Kate fully intended on saying aloud, but Aila just rolled right over her.

"No sarcasm or excuses. Kátheryn forced you to take that first step in accepting who you were, and in doing so, you disrupted time. Which, of course, brought down Durlan's wrath. Then there was my winter intent on ending you, along with James's own curse that grew because of your continued absence. Do you think all this was just happenstance?"

Well, put like that—it really started to sound like everyone was trying to manipulate her into making mistakes, screwing up... and then, oh-so-kindly, just slapped a full-on blame with her name attached to it.

Aila lifted her hands to the summer, the sun and its glinting wink at her as it set in those dark, far off mountains.

"And yet, look where we are. Look who *you* are now." She waved her pale hand at Kate.

Not that Kate needed her to. Oh, no. She felt the difference. Hell, she'd *seen* the difference ever since she'd stepped out of the glade. Her magic waking up. Her dual flames becoming one and then,

then this... using the larch tree and its light that, yes, *had* been frozen in time.

Not to mention, she hadn't once slipped and fallen on her ass while running across Aila's ice field.

Kate took a deep breath. It was a bit much to take in. Then, let it back out.

"All this," she said, "all this happened to wake me up."

"To get you to finally accept who you are."

"You still tried to kill me."

"Yes. I'm sure it won't be the last time, either. I still wish you'd never have gone near my son."

Well, if that was one thing about Aila, she was always pretty up front and honest with her feelings about Kate. And it meant things between them were going to be... odd.

Not allies. Not enemies, either.

"And what about the Gathering? What about Severi?" Kate asked.

"They are waiting for us. Waiting for you, anyway, to restart time."

"So that's it? It's all on me."

"It always has been, it seems. Much to my... disappointment."

Yeah, no contest on that one.

But... it still came back to her and her choice.

She could choose to move forward, to accept Aila's help (though no way in hell would she ever fully trust it), or... she could leave her here.

Leave her trapped in time, and oh, believe her, Kate knew she could.

It was that sense again, that little tingling of awareness. Of the way her breath sparked out of her and the warmth, the heat of her flames danced just underneath her skin.

It had been her magic that brought them both here, and it would be her magic, and hers alone, that would get them both home.

Aila knew it, too. And even still, she'd given the choice... to Kate. Left it for Kate to decide.

The truth was, Aila had probably revealed a whole hell lot more than she'd ever wanted to when she was the Snow Queen and all. Her cold, raging anger... she probably couldn't control what she'd said, not really, certainly not how she felt about it (and Kate). She'd wanted another elf-descendant with Kátheryn's soul, someone who she *could* shape and control, as she'd tried to do with James. In fact, Aila was probably doing her darnedest right now pretending like none of that mattered, that it had just been her under Severi's spell and that's all it was. To not pay much attention to those pesky little details... like her being royalty and dead-set on killing Kate.

But Kate had been paying attention, and gosh darn it, she *was* learning.

And learning how to play this little elf-and-mouse game, or whatever the hell it was.

Regardless, this was where they stood.

In a summer, one paused out of time, sweating in some pretty heavy winter clothes (at least, Kate anyway), surrounded by the most beautiful wildflowers Kate had ever seen, and amongst them, the remnants of her larch tree and the price of all this had been to get her to this place, to this time.

To accepting who she was.

Along with... Aila. Not enemies. Not allies.

Again, she could leave Aila here, would never have to worry about her again, and the temptation... it was there. Just like it was there to use the time magic to make that happen. Again, for her own purpose.

And it'd be so easy, too.

Except, could she live with herself? Truly? And could she live with the consequences? Because if there was one thing she'd learned, there were always consequences.

The answer was simple:

No.

No, she couldn't.

And she also couldn't leave James's mother, bitch though she was (not to mention the two trees she'd tried to squash her with), but Kate couldn't leave her here. Not and still be the person that she was.

Kate took another deep breath. The soothing mountain air, that freshness, crisp and clear, the moist earth underneath her feet. All of it, so real, all of it feeling like home.

But it was time to go.

Time to fix what she'd promised to fix. And Aila needed Kate, and much as she hated to admit it, she needed Aila. If nothing else but to *unpause* time again. Cause really, an instruction manual would seriously be nice about now.

But then again... maybe she didn't need Aila's help. Kate had gotten this far on her own, she could figure out how to get back.

All she had to do was listen... and to trust... in herself.

"Okay," Kate said. "Let's go home. Together."

Aila nodded. "Thank you."

"You have a lot to make up for."

Aila merely held out her hand in answer, and after a healthy moment of thought and distrust, Kate took it. Their fingers touching, oh so lightly, Kate focused on her dual flames, their unique colors and the way they blended together just so...

Her magic.

Hers and hers alone.

She felt herself fall back into time, felt that whoosh of magic, that slight step between worlds, as she passed through the veil, the cold, chilling touch of shadows as they kissed her cheeks, her forehead, almost like a promise that yes, she would be back and one day... one day soon...

And then felt the unmistakable pull of James and the ribbon they shared. That glowing gold, how it shined, shined so bright there was no mistaking the way home.

She followed their ribbon...

And her feet, winter boots and all, touched back down onto a ground that hadn't an inch of snow but was covered by the same beautiful wildflowers. A sea of them, at the tail-end of summer, all purples and blues and reds. And right alongside them were the shriveled, brown leaves of her larch tree.

A reminder.

A promise.

"Thank you," she whispered, "I'll remember."

The wind again came, still cold, still carrying a chill that wasn't just gonna go away because she'd broken the winter spell on Aila. It picked up the last of the larch's leaves and then they were gone. Soaring off into the sky, a sky so blue now, so high and wide, it looked like it could go on forever.

And probably did.

Then, finally, the unmistakable cry of an eagle. Her eagle. Not soaring overhead like before, but inside her.

Right inside her heart.

Right where he'd been this whole time, right where her magic had been. All the answers she'd needed. Waiting for her to finally accept herself. To finally believe.

And she did.

Find your home. Find your heart.

Searching for Sanctuary: An Enchantment Avenue Novel, on sale now from your favorite retailer. Turn the page for a sample chapter from that book.

Aisha Faye leans against the hot, chain-link fence of the cage, one of many in her waystation for unwanted, magical creatures. She watches, helplessly, as a tiger once overflowing with magic now lays there unresponsive.

No joy. No spark. Slowly dying.

Just like all the others.

Across town, in the world of elite witches and wizards, Nate Darkwood watches the same.

Both Aisha and Nate need answers with only way to find them: together.

A novel set in the dazzling world of Enchantment Avenue. *Searching for Sanctuary,* a story of hope and redemption, love and magic... and all of them, possible.

Aisha leaned against the cage's rusted chain-link fence. The hot surface heated her dark skin, but she ignored it.

The tiger Lanhi lay sprawled and uncaring on her wooden hovel of a house's flat roof. Massive paw hanging off. Not even swinging in the nonexistent breeze. Not the way she used to, like she was batting at some stray hopping-kangaroo mouse that'd wandered in from the southern pen enclosures.

It'd only happened once, not long after Lanhi had arrived, when she'd barely had the will to even eat her food. Aisha hadn't respelled the mouse enclosure lock against hair-thin whisker-picking abilities (the hopping-kangaroo mouse's master having not informed Aisha of their peculiar talents—the same talents that'd gotten them banned from hearth and home and a much nicer, much more expensive Familiar Sanctuary).

But the little adventure of hopping-kangaroo mice had given Lanhi (and the mice) some of their own spark back. Both sides had survived (thank goodness), and while the doors were now safely locked and secure, the spark had held.

Especially for Lanhi.

Until today.

Until whatever had made her change, made her revert back to the tiger with barely the will to live.

And yet, even now Lanhi lay on her roof with her paw hanging down as if the memory of the mice was still with her. Still hanging on. Perhaps even a small spark remained for her to be on guard for the next silly hopping-kangaroo mouse foolish enough to come into her domain of faded and tearing circus posters, elephant stands, and flung-about clown noses on the dust-dirt floor of her enclosure.

Even though her paw just hung there. Unmoving. Uncaring.

"Come on, sweetheart. Please." Aisha felt the magic within her gut stir. Slowly, as if reaching out to the tiger...testing and unsure.

Aisha held her breath.

She hoped Marcelle had reported wrong. Hoped her magic would prove otherwise, that their dancing Lanhi was fine.

Lanhi ruffed and grumped. A hot puff of air spewed from her massive mouth of teeth and tongue, blowing at the tattered, pale-pink tutu hanging from a skirt hook.

The sparkly sequins, no longer sparkly.

The ruffles wrinkled and limp.

The tutu had been a recent addition. As had the clown noses. Insisted by Lanhi's master, the witch Ghazille.

Fat lot of good that had done Lanhi.

The unrelenting Simi Valley sun beat down on Aisha, the outside cage, the lines and lines of other Familiar cages in her Waystation, barely a narrow, dirt footpath between them. Even the tiniest movement caused a small twister of dust to billow upwards. The dust didn't even spare poor Lanhi, her no longer shimmering, no longer carefully groomed orange-, white-, and black-striped coat and instead, now dull and faded. The Waystation's famous dust coated every surface, made Aisha's skin look a pale tan instead of the dark, sun-kissed skin of her grandfather's people, the Hadzabe tribe.

A tribe she couldn't *actually* remember.

Aisha snapped her eyes closed. Squeezed them shut.

She needed to focus on Lanhi. Focus on someone she *could* help.

Who *wanted* help.

Sweat trickled down Aisha's forehead. Dripped off her nose. She didn't move. Not even when the salty sweat slid into the corner of her eye.

Any movement, sudden or even slow, could send the tiger Familiar into another set of fits.

It was one of the main reasons Lanhi had been banned from her previous sanctuary. An uncontrollable Familiar was a handful; an unpredictable one, a danger to everyone. The kind of Familiar those high-end Sanctuaries didn't want to help.

But Aisha did.

Her magic continued to circle. To rise up from her chest, reaching her throat. Still tentative. Unsure. Trying desperately to reach out, to find some connection between Aisha and Lanhi, something that would help her understand—would help the tiger keep wanting to live.

She almost wished Lanhi would have those fits again. Anything to bring the tiger back to her usual spirits. Anything at all to show that she wasn't withering away.

Just like so many of the other retired, abused, and often forgotten Familiars.

Lanhi ruffed again. Blew another a sigh of hot air. Made the tutu's ruffles dance just the slightest, but nothing like the way those ruffles had danced before Lanhi had been sent to the finest Familiar sanctuary in the Northern Hemisphere, Paradise Grove Familiar sanctuary— before, of course, coming to Aisha's barely-holding-together Waystation.

There wasn't even the tiniest bit of excitement behind those hooded orange-gold eyes.

The magic in Aisha's stomach settled into a cold, hard stone.

Not even a stirring remained.

"Damn," Aisha whispered. "Not another one."

Aisha swept off her felt-brimmed cowboy hat. Slapped it against her khaki pants. Dust billowed up and into her nose, tickled it. Right alongside the tang of animals and sweat, rotting meat, and just plain hot-dry Waystation.

She sneezed. Then sneezed again.

Felt a familiar ache for home, a longing to go back to another time. Funny how a sneeze could remind her of the hot summers at her parents' thriving sanctuary in the Serengeti Magical Proper. Back when her life was going just fine and climbing upwards, upwards to where no sky, no magic was the limit.

She slapped the hat back on her head.

She'd never change that clock, though.

Never.

This was exactly where she needed to be.

Who she needed to be.

Aisha gave one last look at Lanhi. She'd have to call the witch, Ghazille. Not that the woman would care. Not that any of them did, not after their Familiars wound up in the Waystation, the last stop on their abandoned, unhappy, and too often short lives.

At least for these Familiars.

Not all Familiars led the perfect lives the Enchantment Avenue Council (hell, even that great and powerful High Council) liked to preach from their safe havens of magic and strength. They pretended ignorance when it came to abuse and misuse of Familiars, turning a blind eye especially when it came to the highest among them.

But Aisha knew better, and so did the Enchantment Avenue Council.

Her Waystation was living proof, and they knew it, too. Did their best to keep it all under wraps. An open, unacknowledged secret.

Even if they needed her.

Needed someone to take in the Familiars who couldn't handle the strain of performing like a monkey for unrelenting magical masters. The kinds of masters who didn't even deserve a pet, let alone the special, magical bond shared with a Familiar.

An old argument, though.

She sighed, knowing there was nothing she could do. Not about the Council and not for Lanhi. And all the Familiars like her.

But she wouldn't let them go out alone.

Whatever it took, she'd be there for them.

To continue reading, *Searching for Sanctuary*, visit ChrissyWissler.com or your favorite bookseller.

bowl of ice cream. Double-scoop of huckleberry, cookies n' cream, sprinkles, river of hot fudge.

No problems at all.

Except for her backpack zinging with magic. And the impatient, unhappy tree tapping at her window.

Ignore an angry forest? Not a good idea.

Hidden in Darkness, a story about a reluctant girl coming to terms with herself and the magic living inside her—whether or not she wants it. The "In-Between" Elven Heritage Story, set some time after the events in *Hidden in Time*.

By joining my list you'll receive wonderful benefits such as being notified of upcoming book releases as well as the never-before-published short story and special gift for fans of the series: *Hidden in Darkness*.

To enjoy your free copy of *Hidden in Darkness* and keep up with the latest news and releases, go to https://dl.bookfunnel.com/yk3ksnyz29 and chrissywissler.com.

ABOUT THE AUTHOR

Chrissy Wissler's writing has garnered praise both from readers and professional writers. Readers love her characters and the emotional grip she engenders.

About her novel *Home Run*, *New York Times* bestselling author Kristine Kathryn Rusch said: "Wonderful book, chockfull of unexpected surprises. If you like sports novels, you'll like this—even if you don't like romance. If you like romance, you'll like this—even if you don't like sports novels."

Chrissy's short fiction has appeared in the anthologies: *Fiction River: Risk-Takers, Fiction River Presents: Legacies, Fiction River Presents: Readers' Choice, Deep Magic,* and *When Dreams Come True.* She writes fantasy and science fiction, as well as a softball, contemporary series for both romance and young adult.

Before turning to fiction, Chrissy also wrote nonfiction for publications such as *Montana Outdoors, Women in the Outdoors,* and *Jakes Magazine.* In 2009, *Inside Kung Fu* magazine awarded her with their 'Writer of the Year' award.

Follow her online at ChrissyWissler.com, as well as her blog on being a parent-writer, at ParentsandProse.com.

To enjoy another story by Chrissy Wissler and to keep up with the latest news, releases and more, go to: chrissywissler.com/free-book/

For more information:
www.chrissywissler.com
chrissy@chrissywissler.com

ALSO BY CHRISSY WISSLER

Elven Heritage Series

Hidden in Mist

Hidden in Truth

Hidden in Shadow

Hidden in Fire

Hidden in Flight

Hidden in Spirit

Hidden in Desire

Hidden in Memory

Hidden in Time Novel

Hidden in Lore: Collection #1

Hidden in Myth: Collection #2

Hidden in Legend: Collection #3

Hidden in Darkness: Free Story

Little League Series

Swing Away: A Little League Novel

Prom Dates & Softball Bats

Throw Like a Girl, Catch a Date

Fly Away

No Crying in Softball

More to Life than Softball

A Pitcher's Unexpected Date

A Catcher's Christmas Wish

Stolen Bases, Stolen Kisses

Softball Baby

Off-Balance

Batter-Up Pucker-Up: Collection

Everlasting: Collection

All or Nothing: Collection

Home Run Series

Home Run

Romance Video Game Series

Second Chance: Novel

Anything Possible

Enchantment Avenue

Searching for Sanctuary: Novel

Dragons in Preschool: Short Novel

The Blessings Bridge

Pixie Dust Cupcakes

Christmas Weather Witch

Unfreeze a Heart

More than Nurture

www.ingramcontent.com/pod-product-compliance
Lightning Source LLC
Chambersburg PA
CBHW051702180726
48283CB00004B/1177